THE HOUSEKEEPER'S AWAKENING

BY

SHARON KENDRICK

MILLS & BOON

First published in Great Britain 2014
by Mills & Boon, an imprint of Harlequin (UK) Limited,
Large Print edition 2015
Eton House, 18-24 Paradise Road,
Richmond, Surrey, TW9 1SR

 © 2014 Sharon Kendrick

ISBN: 978-0-263-25582-9

Printed and bound in Great Britain
by CPI Antony Rowe, Chippenham, Wiltshire

With special thanks to
George Tilbury and Erika Ring,
for teaching me how bodies heal.

Also, for invaluable insights into the world
of motor racing, thank you to Keith Roberts
and team-owner Roland Dane.
Roland, in particular, helped breathe life
into Luis Martinez!

And to Peter Crone
for his invaluable help with wind-farms
(although they appear in Murat's book—
SEDUCED BY THE SULTAN!)

CHAPTER ONE

CARLY'S FINGERS STILLED as the angry voice echoed through the house like a low rumble of thunder.

'Carly!'

She stared at the cornstarch which had lodged itself under her fingernails.

Now what?

She supposed she could try ignoring him but what would be the point? When her fractious, brilliant, mercurial boss wanted something he wanted it ten minutes ago; preferably sooner. He was driven, committed and single-minded— even when operating at fifty per cent of his usual capacity. It was just that fifty per cent of Luis Martinez's capacity would be full throttle for most men.

She pulled a face. Hadn't he already disrupted

the peace enough times over the last few weeks
with his incessant orders and his bad temper?
She supposed that he'd had a pretty good reason to be more demanding than usual, but even
so… She had lost count of the times she'd been
forced to bite her tongue, when he'd snapped
out yet another arrogant command. Maybe that
quicksilver mind of his would focus on something else if she pretended she hadn't heard him.
Maybe if she wished hard enough, he might just
go away and leave her alone.

Preferably for ever.

'Carly!'

Maybe not. The shout had grown even more
impatient now, so she took off her apron and
shook her ponytail free. Quickly washing her
hands, she set off towards the gym complex
at the back of the house, where Luis Enrique
Gabriel Martinez was currently undergoing
another rehabilitation session with his physiotherapist.

Or rather, rehabilitation was what he was
supposed to be doing, following the car crash

which everyone said he'd been lucky to survive. Lately, Carly had wondered if the daily sessions had slipped over the boundary from the professional to the personal. Which might explain why the previously cool physiotherapist had started adding significant amounts of make-up before her visits, and spraying herself with a cloud of gingery-lemon scent just before she rang the doorbell. But that was par for the course, wasn't it? Luis had something special when it came to women. Something to do with those rugged South American looks and an unquenchable appetite for life which frequently courted danger.

Luis came, saw and conquered—though not necessarily in that order. He had an unerring ability to turn women into puddles of meek surrender, even if he happened to be lying stricken on a hospital bed at the time. Hadn't half the nurses who had treated him turned up here after he'd discharged himself? They had trooped through the door, bearing nervous smiles and sad little bunches of grapes—along with some pretty flimsy excuses about why they were visiting. But Carly had known exactly why they were visiting. A bed-bound and very sexy billionaire was an irresistible target, though to her surprise he'd given them all short shrift—even the platinum blonde with the legs which seemed to go all the way up to her armpits.

Carly was just grateful to be one of the few women immune to the Argentinian's careless charm, even if the truth of it was that he'd never actually *tried* to charm her. Maybe that was one of the advantages of being known as a dedicated 'plain Jane'—that your sex god of a boss would inevitably look through you as if you were part of the wallpaper. Which left her free to do her job and work towards a brighter future. And to remind herself of Luis's many negative qualities: his selfishness, restlessness and disregard for his own safety—as well as his annoying habit of leaving tiny espresso cups all around the house, which she was always finding in the most unexpected places.

She reached the gym complex and hesitated

for a moment, wondering if it might be better to wait until he had finished his massage.

'Carly!'

Had he heard her approaching, even though in these old sneakers her footsteps were practically silent? She knew it was said of Luis Martinez that his senses were as finely tuned as his cars and one of the reasons why he had dominated the racing scene for so long.

Still she hesitated.

'Carly, will you stop skulking around outside the door and get yourself in here!'

His raised tone was arrogant and peremptory and she guessed that some people would have found it offensive to be spoken to in such a way, but Carly was used to Luis Martinez by now. She knew what his entourage said about him. That his bark was worse than his bite. Though she wasn't sure if that bit was strictly true. His last but one girlfriend had seemed rather *fond* of his bite. Why else would she have kept appearing at breakfast during her brief tenure as his lover sporting bruises on her neck with a kind of joyful pride, as if she'd spent the night with some obliging vampire?

Knowing that she couldn't put it off any longer, Carly opened the gym door and walked into the room where her famous employer was lying on his back on the narrow massage table. His dark head was pillowed on his clasped hands and his golden-olive body was outlined against the white sheet. His gaze alighted on her and his black eyes narrowed with something which looked like relief.

Which was weird. She thought that they tolerated each other pretty well, but there wasn't what you'd call any real *affection* between them.

Or maybe it was not so weird after all. Quickly, she became aware of the tension in the room and of two things which couldn't go unnoticed. That Mary Houghton, the physiotherapist, was standing on the far side of the room breathing rather heavily as she stared fixedly down at her shoes. And that Luis was completely naked, save for the trio of small white towels which were strategically placed at his groin.

A wave of colour swept into Carly's face and suddenly she felt angry. Wouldn't it have been polite for him to have covered up before she arrived? Surely he must have known that it simply wasn't done to greet a member of your staff in such a way. That she might find it...*embarrassing* to see that rippling chest and broad shoulders on display. Or that it was *arrogant* to flaunt those long, bare legs, which were currently sprawled out in front of him?

She kept away from men and all their complications—and with good reason. Experience had made her wary; but for once, all her latent fears and hang-ups about the opposite sex were put on hold as she stared at her boss with reluctant fascination.

Looking at him now, it was easy to see why women adored him. Why the newspapers had nicknamed him The Love Machine, when he'd been at the peak of his powers, and motor-racing champion of the world. Before her time, of course, but Carly had heard of him, even then. Everyone had.

His face had been everywhere—on or off the track. When he hadn't been standing on podiums, garlanded in the winner's laurels and spraying champagne over the adoring crowds, he had been an advertiser's dream. Magnified images of Luis Martinez wearing expensive watches, with that famously devil-may-care smile on his face, were regularly emblazoned over giant billboards. Off-duty, his fascination had been equally compelling. Hunky South American billionaires always provided good copy—especially as he was rarely seen without the requisite blonde clinging possessively to his arm. And if some perceptive journalist had once remarked that his jet-dark eyes looked almost *empty*—perhaps that only added to his appeal.

Because Luis Martinez wasn't just good-looking—even Carly recognised that. There was something *wild* about him. Something untamed. He was the trophy which was always just out of reach. The desired object which no woman could hold onto for long. That mane of slightly too-long black hair gave him a reckless, buccaneering look and those black eyes were now studying her in a way which was making her feel distinctly uncomfortable.

Turning away from his scrutiny, she looked at Mary Houghton, who had been coming to his English mansion for weeks now. With her neat figure and shiny hair, the physiotherapist looked as pretty as she always did in her crisp white uniform, but Carly thought she could see a shadow of hurt clouding the other woman's features.

'So there you are, Carly,' said Luis, his voice heavy with sarcasm. 'At last. Did you fly in from the opposite side of the world to get here? You know I don't like to be kept waiting.'

'I was busy making *alfajores*,' said Carly. 'For you to have with your coffee later.'

'Ah, yes.' He gave her a grudging nod. 'Your timekeeping may be abysmal, but nobody can deny that you're an excellent cook. And your *alfajores* are as good as those which I used to eat when I was growing up.'

'Was there something special you wanted?'

questioned Carly pointedly. 'Because this particular kind of baking doesn't lend itself kindly
to interruptions.'

'As the world's worst timekeeper, I don't think
you're in a position to lecture me on time man-
agement,' he snapped, turning his head to look
at Mary Houghton, who for some reason had
gone very red. 'I sometimes think Carly for-
gets that a certain degree of submissiveness is
a desirable quality in a housekeeper. But she is
undoubtedly capable and so I am prepared to
tolerate her occasional insubordination. Do you
think she can do it, Mary—can someone like
her get me back to my fighting best, now that
you are intent on leaving me?'

By now, Carly had stopped thinking about
the Argentinian cakes which were Luis's favou-
rites, or his arrogant sense of entitlement. She
was too interested in the fraught atmosphere to
even object to being talked about as if she were
an inanimate object. She wanted to know why
the previously cool physiotherapist was now

chewing on her lip as if something awful had happened.

Had it?

'Is something wrong?' she asked.

Mary Houghton gave Carly a lukewarm smile accompanied by an awkward shrug of her shoulders. 'Not exactly…wrong. But my professional association with Señor Martinez has…come to an end. He no longer requires the services of a physiotherapist,' she said, and for a moment her voice sounded a little unsteady. 'But he will continue to need massage and exercise for the next few weeks on a regular basis to ensure a complete recovery, and someone needs to oversee that.'

'Right,' said Carly uncertainly, because she couldn't see where all this was leading.

Luis fixed her with a piercing look, his black eyes boring into her like twin lasers. 'You wouldn't have a problem taking over from Mary for a while, would you, Carly? You're pretty good with your hands, aren't you?'

'Me?' The word came out as a horrified croak.

'Why not?'

Carly's eyes widened, because suddenly all her fears didn't seem so latent any more. The thought of going anywhere near a half-naked man was making her skin crawl—even if that man *was* Luis Martinez. She swallowed. 'You mean, I'd be expected to *massage* you?'

Now there was a definite glint in his eyes and she couldn't work out if it was displeasure or amusement. 'Why, is that such an *abhorrent* thought to you, Carly?'

'No, no, of course not.' But it was. Of course it was. Wouldn't he laugh out loud if he realised how little she knew about men? Wouldn't she be the last person he'd choose as his temporary masseuse, if he knew what a naïve innocent she was? So should she tell him the truth—if not all of it, then at least some?

Of course she should tell him!

She shrugged her shoulders, aware of the heightened rush of colour to her cheeks as she mumbled out the words. 'It's just that I've…

well, I've never actually given anyone a massage before.'

'Oh, that won't be a problem.' Mary Houghton's cool accent cut through Carly's stumbled explanation. 'I can show you the basic technique—it isn't difficult. If you're good with your hands, you won't have a problem with it. The exercises—ditto. They're easy enough to pick up and Señor Martinez already knows how to do them properly. The most important thing you can do is to ensure he keeps to a regular schedule.'

'Think you can do it, Carly?'

The silky South American voice filtered through the air and as Carly turned, the intensity of his gaze suddenly made her feel *dizzy*. And uncomfortable. It was as if he'd never really looked at her properly before. Or at least, not like that. She got the feeling that he had always regarded her as one of the fixtures and fittings—like one of the squashy velvet sofas which he sometimes lay on in the evenings if he'd brought a woman back here. But now his eyes were almost...*calculating* and she felt a stab of alarm as he assessed her. Was he thinking what countless men had doubtless thought before? That she was plain and awkward and didn't make the best of herself. Would it surprise him to know that she liked it that way? That she *liked* to fade into the background? Because life was safer that way. Safer and more predictable.

Pushing away the nudge of dark memories with an efficiency born of years of practice, she considered his question. Of course she could learn how to massage him because—as he'd just said—she was very good with her hands. She ran his English home like clockwork, didn't she? She cooked and cleaned and made sure the Egyptian cotton sheets were softly ironed whenever he was in residence. She arranged for caterers to arrive if he was hosting a big party, or for prize-winning chefs to be ferried down from London if he was holding a more intimate gathering. She had florists on speed dial, ready to deck his house with fragrant blooms at the drop of a hat or to float candle-topped lilies in his outdoor pool, if the weather remained fine enough.

What she wished she had the courage to say was that she didn't *want* to do it. That the thought of going anywhere near his body was making her feel...*peculiar*. And even though her dream of being a doctor was what kept her in this fairly mundane job—she didn't want her first experience of the therapeutic to be with a man with the reputation of Luis Martinez.

Imagine having to touch his skin, especially if he was barely covered by a few meagre towels, as he was at the moment. Imagine being closeted alone in the massage room with him, day after day. Having to put up with his short fuse and bad temper in such an intimate setting. Luis Martinez she could cope with, yes, but preferably with as much distance between them as possible.

'Surely there must be somebody else who could do it?' she said.

'But I don't want anyone else doing it—I

want you,' he said. 'Or do you have other things which are occupying you, Carly? Things which are making too many demands on your time and which will prevent you from spending time doing what I am asking you to do? Is there something I should know about? After all, I *am* the one paying your salary, aren't I?'

Carly's hands balled into two fists, because now he had her in a corner and they both knew it. He paid her a staggeringly generous amount of money, most of which she squirrelled away towards her goal of getting to med school.

She had the cushiest of positions here, which left her plenty of time to study. As jobs went, she would go so far as to say she loved working here. She loved it most when Luis was out of the country, which was most of the time. He had gorgeous homes in far-flung corners of the world, sited wherever he had business interests, and his English residence was usually bottom on his list of visits. She wasn't even sure why he bothered keeping this vast, country house until one day she had summoned up the courage to ask his burly assistant, Diego. 'Tax,' had been the ex-wrestler's terse reply.

Carly's role was to keep the house in a constant state of readiness in case Luis should decide to pay an unexpected visit. In fact, he wouldn't be here now were it not for the charity car race which she thought he'd been insane to enter and which had ended with him smashing his pelvis and spending weeks in hospital.

She looked at him—thinking about his general high-handedness and arrogance and whether she would be able to tolerate it on a far more intimate basis. How could she possibly massage him without giving into the temptation to sink her fingernails into that silken olive flesh of his and make him squirm? How on earth would she be able to *touch* such a notorious sex god, without making a complete and utter fool of herself?

'I just wonder whether you might be better getting another professional in,' she said stubbornly.

He flicked a glance at Mary Houghton, who was still standing in exactly the same position and Carly saw his mouth twist with undisguised irritation. 'Can you give us a moment, please, Mary?'

'Of course I can. I'll…I'll talk to you when you've finished in here, Carly.' There was a pause, before Mary held her hand out. 'Goodbye, Luis. It's been…well, it's been great.'

He nodded, but Carly thought how *cold* his face looked as he propped himself up on one elbow, before shaking the physiotherapist's hand. Whatever Mary had said or done had not pleased him.

'Goodbye, Mary,' he said.

There was silence as she left the room and Luis sat up—impatiently gesturing for Carly to hand him the robe hanging from a hook on the back of the door.

She did as he wanted—quickly averting her eyes until he'd covered up with the black towelling robe, but when he spoke, he still sounded irritated.

'Why are you so reluctant to do what I ask?'

he demanded. 'Why are you being so damned stubborn?'

For a moment Carly didn't answer. Would he scoff if he knew that his proposed intimacy scared her? Or would he just be shocked to learn that she had allowed one horrendous experience to colour her judgement—and she'd spent her life running away from the kind of personal contact which most women of her age considered perfectly natural? Someone like Luis would probably tell her to 'move on', in the way that people did—as if it were that easy.

And this was about more than what had happened to her, wasn't it? She could see nothing but trouble if she agreed, because rich and powerful men like Luis *were* trouble. Hadn't her own sister been chasing that kind of man ever since she'd first sprouted breasts, and didn't she keep on going back for more—despite getting knocked back, time after time?

Thoughts of Bella's inglorious escapades flitted through her mind as she met Luis's luminous gaze. 'I don't want to neglect my house-keeping duties,' she said.

'Then get somebody else to do the cooking and the cleaning instead of you. How difficult can it be?'

Carly flushed. She knew that housekeeping wasn't up there with being a lawyer or a doctor, but she still found it faintly humiliating to hear Luis dismiss her job quite so flippantly.

'Or get in a professional masseuse who could do it better than I ever could?' she suggested again.

'No,' he said, almost viciously. 'I'm sick of strangers. Sick of people with different agendas, coming into my house and telling me what I must and mustn't do.' His mouth hardened into a forbidding line. 'What's the matter, Carly? Are you objecting on the basis that providing massage for your recuperating boss isn't written into your contract?'

'I haven't got a contract,' she said bluntly.

'You haven't?'

'No. You told me when I interviewed for the

job that if I didn't trust you to give me your word, then you weren't the kind of person you wanted working for you.'

An arrogant smile spread over his lips. 'Did I really say that?'

'Yes. You did.' And she had accepted his terms, hadn't she, even if the logical side of her brain had told her that she'd been a fool to do so? In fact, she'd practically bitten his hand off, because she had recognised that Luis Martinez was offering her the kind of opportunity which wasn't going to come her way again. A place to live and a salary big enough to make substantial savings for her future.

The smile had now left his lips.

'I am growing bored with this discussion,' he snapped. 'Are you prepared to help me out or not?'

She recognised the implicit threat behind his words. Help me out or else.

Or else what?

Go out and find a new job? One which wouldn't leave her with so much free time to study for her exams? She frowned as she thought about the champagne bill from his last party and a new resolve filled her.

'I'd be prepared to do it, if you were prepared to give me some sort of bonus,' she said suddenly.

'Danger money, you mean?' he mocked. With a grimace he swung his long legs over the side of the massage bed, but not before Carly had seen a peek of hair-roughened thigh as the robe flapped open.

'Yes, that's right. Danger money,' she croaked, quickly averting her gaze once more. 'I couldn't have put it better myself.'

He gave a short laugh. 'Funny. I never really had you down as a negotiator, Carly.'

'Oh? And why's that?'

Luis didn't answer immediately, just concentrated on stretching his hips, the way that Mary had shown him. He wouldn't bother telling his plain little housekeeper that she had merely confirmed his belief that everyone had a price, because that might upset her, and there was no point in upsetting a woman if it could possibly be avoided. Often, of course, it couldn't. Usually because they weren't listening to what you were saying, or they thought they could change your mind for you.

Or they started falling in love with you, even though you hadn't given them the slightest encouragement to do so. His mouth hardened. That had been Mary Houghton's mistake. He'd seen it growing day by day, until in the end she could barely look at him without blushing. She'd made it clear that she was keen for a... *liaison* and, yes, he'd been tempted. Of course he had. She was a good-looking woman and hadn't he read somewhere that physiotherapists made great lovers because they knew how the body worked? But it had been highly unprofessional of her, and some deep-rooted and rather old-fashioned prejudice against such things had appalled him.

He turned his attention back to Carly. At least in her he had nothing to fear because sexual attraction was unlikely to rear its head. He found himself wondering if she bothered keeping a mirror in her bedroom, or whether she just didn't see what the rest of the world saw.

Her thick brown hair was tugged back from her face in a ponytail and she wore no make-up. He'd never seen mascara on those pale lashes which framed eyes the colour of iced tea, nor lipstick on her sometimes disapproving lips. A little blusher would have added some much-needed colour to her pale skin, and he'd often wondered why she insisted on wearing a plain blue overall during working hours. To protect her clothes, she said—though, from the glimpses he'd caught of them, hers were not the kind of clothes which looked as if they needed much in the way of protection. Weren't man-made fabrics notoriously hard-wearing? They were also very unflattering when stretched tightly over unfashionably curvy bodies like hers.

Luis was used to women who turned femininity into an art form. Who invested vast amounts of time and money making themselves look beautiful, then spent the rest of their lives trying to preserve that state of being. But not this one. Oh, no. Definitely not this one.

His lips flattened into a wry smile. What was it that the English said? Never to judge a book by its cover. And the old adage did have some truth in it—because despite her plainness and total lack of adornment, nobody could deny that Carly Conner had spirit. He could think of no other woman who would have hesitated for more than a second at the thought of—literally—getting their hands on him. Which of course was precisely the reason why he wanted her for the job. He needed to get fit, and he needed to do it as quickly as possible—because this inactivity was driving him crazy.

All he wanted was to feel normal again. He loathed the world passing him by, so that all he could do was watch it. Because inactivity left you with time to think. It left you feeling as if something was missing. He wanted to get back on the ski slopes. He wanted to pilot a plane again. He wanted the challenge of dangerous sports to fill him with adrenaline and make him feel alive again.

His mouth twisted as he levered himself off the bed.

'Hand me my crutches, will you, Carly?'

She raised her eyebrows.

He gave a small growl. 'Please.'

Silently, Carly handed them over and watched as he grasped them, straightening up to his full and impressive height. It still seemed strange to see a man as powerful as Luis needing crutches, but at least he was well on the road to recovery now. Almost unscathed, he had come through an accident the doctors said he'd been lucky to survive.

He hadn't raced professionally for five years, but the lure of an enormous charity prize organised by one of the big car manufacturers had proved too much to resist. That, and an inbuilt arrogance that he was indestructible…and a nature which loved to embrace danger in its many forms.

She remembered the day it had happened,

when she'd received the phone call to say he'd been rushed to hospital. Her heart had been racing as she had driven through the narrow country roads, reaching the accident and emergency department and fearing the worst, to be told that he'd been taken to Theatre and they weren't sure how bad it was.

His entourage had been going crazy. There had been people rushing around all over the place and getting in the way of the medical staff. Security people. PR people. Diego, his swarthy assistant, had been dealing with the press, and his lawyers were busily engaged with threats of litigation, claiming that the racetrack had been unsafe.

Carly wondered if any of them had actually remembered that they were all there because a man was sick and wounded. And that was when her old pattern of wanting to care had kicked in. She had crept upstairs to the intensive care unit, where the nurse had let her sit with him and everyone else had been barred, on the grounds that any more excitement might hinder his recovery. She remembered thinking how *alone* he looked, despite all his money and success. There had been no family to visit. His parents were dead and he had no brothers or sisters. Carly had been the only one there for him.

All that night she had stayed put, holding his motionless hand and running her fingertips over it. Telling the unresponsive figure who dominated the narrow hospital gurney that he was going to be okay. But the experience had been a strangely powerful one. It had been a shock to see him looking so *vulnerable* and for a short while Carly's feelings towards her irascible boss had undergone a slight transformation. For a while she had felt almost *tender* towards him…

Until he had started recovering and had become his usual arrogant self. She had been elbowed out of the way then, when the first of a long stream of women had arrived, all vying with each other in their tiny leather miniskirts— because everyone knew that the ex-world champion was turned on by leather. She remembered turning up at the ward one day to find a stunning blonde in thigh-high boots groping him under the bed-sheet. And Carly hadn't bothered visiting again. She hadn't seen him again until he'd discharged himself home against his doctors' advice.

But she suspected that the accident had changed him, as she knew that near-fatal accidents sometimes did. Even though the house was vast, it had seemed overcrowded with his people mooching around the place, not sure what to do with themselves while their boss was recovering. And Luis had been even more bad-tempered than usual. He hadn't liked people trailing in and out of his room to speak to him, saying that it made him feel like a dying king. Demanding peace, he had sent his entire entourage back to Buenos Aires—even Diego. Carly remembered their astonishment at being sent packing. And hers. Because once again, Luis Martinez really was on his own. Only this time, he was alone with *her*.

Emerging from her silent reverie, she realised that his eyes were trained on her and that he was waiting for the answer to a question which, in reality, was little more than an order.

'Yes, I'll do it.' She sighed. 'I'd better go and talk to Mary and get her to run over exactly what it is you need, though I don't know why you couldn't just have carried on paying for her to see you privately.'

She soon discovered why, when she found Mary Houghton in the garden room, staring rigidly out of the French windows at the rain-soaked gardens outside. The bright hues of the summer flowers looked like fragments of a shattered rainbow, but all Carly could see was that the physiotherapist's shoulders were shaking slightly.

Was the cool Englishwoman *crying*?

'Mary?' she questioned gently. 'Are you okay?'

It was a few moments before Mary turned round and Carly got her answer from the tell-tale glitter in the other woman's eyes.

'How does he do it, Carly?' Mary questioned in a shaky voice. 'How does he get usually sane women like me to fall for a man they don't even *like*? How come he's dumped me in the coldest way imaginable and I still end up thinking he's the greatest thing since sliced bread?'

Carly tried to crack a joke, anything to lighten the atmosphere and to take that terrible look of *pain* from Mary's face. 'Well, I've never been a great fan of sliced bread myself—which is why I always make my own.'

Mary swallowed. 'I'm sorry. I shouldn't have said anything. Especially not to you. You work for him all the time—you probably deserve my sympathy, instead of me asking for yours.'

'Don't worry about it. You're not the first woman he's reduced to tears and you won't be the last.' Carly shrugged. 'I don't know how he does it, to be honest. I don't think it's calculated, or even intentional. He just seems to have that indefinable something which makes women go crazy for him. Maybe it's inevitable when you're that good-looking and rich and powerful and—'

'Do you know,' interrupted Mary, her voice

suddenly urgent, 'that I've never fancied a male patient before? Never. Not once. The thought had never even crossed my mind—though obviously not many men like Luis Martinez end up on the hospital wards. I can't believe that I allowed him to see it.' She bit her lip. 'It's so… so…*unprofessional*. And so humiliating. And now he's asked me to go, and you know what? I deserve to be let go.'

Carly didn't know what to say. She found herself thinking that things were rarely what they seemed. She'd always thought of Mary Houghton as cool and unflappable. She'd seen her as one of those composed Englishwomen who knew exactly what they were doing and where they were heading. And yet one lazy look from the smouldering black eyes of Luis Martinez and she was as jittery as a schoolgirl who'd just seen her pop-star idol in the flesh.

Carly looked at her. *Maybe she should be glad of the hard lesson she'd learned all those years ago.* Because didn't they say that heartbreak was almost as painful as bereavement? And who in their right mind would want to be going through what the physiotherapist was clearly going through right now?

She looked at Mary. 'I'm sorry,' she said.

Mary pursed her lips together. 'Oh, I'll get over it. And maybe it's all for the best. Maybe I'll start dating that sweet young doctor who's been asking me out for weeks, and forget about a man who's famous for breaking women's hearts. Now,' she said briskly. 'Let me show you what you need to do to get Luis back to full fitness.'

'If you're sure you're okay?'

'Carly, I'm *fine*!'

But Carly noticed Mary delving into her handbag for a tissue and that she blew her nose for a suspiciously long time afterwards.

CHAPTER TWO

CARLY COULD FEEL her heart racing like a train, because this was weird.

It was weirder than weird.

Her hands were unsteady as they positioned themselves above Luis's bare back and she drew in a deep breath, praying he wouldn't guess how nervous she was. Praying that she wouldn't behave like a ham-fisted failure as she began to do exactly what Mary had taught her. It wasn't difficult, she told herself fiercely. Massage was a skill, yes—but it was one that thousands of people did every single day.

But even though the thought of touching Luis's skin was making her mouth grow dry with fear, it seemed there was no way she could avoid it. He was paying her a bonus. They had agreed that this was a deal. And wasn't it crazy to have reached this age and still be scared of touching a man? She lowered her hands towards his gleaming skin and thought about the way she'd let the past impact so profoundly on the present. Was she going to let some worthless piece of scum ruin her life for ever?

Because if she was ever going to fulfil her dream of becoming a doctor, she was going to have to touch people like this every day.

Pressing the heels of her palms deep into his silken flesh, she began to move her hands, glad he couldn't see her face. Wouldn't he laugh himself silly to know that she was flushed with embarrassment?

It was distracting seeing him like this—wearing nothing but a pair of close-fitting black briefs. Catching sight of him and his billionaire buddies lounging around the pool during one of the few hot days last summer while she carried out a tray of drinks was not the same thing at all.

She thought how pale her hands looked against the olive hue of his skin and noticed that her fingers were trembling slightly as they moved over his warm flesh. But to her surprise her nerves soon left her once she got into some kind of rhythm. If she concentrated on the healing aspects of the task, it was easy to push away her uncomfortable thoughts. In a way, it was the opposite of working with pastry, which needed cool, quick movements. For this, her hands were warm and oily and her movements slow and deliberate. She pushed deep into his latissimus dorsi muscles and he gave a little groan.

'Is that okay?' she questioned nervously.

He gave a grunt and she wasn't quite sure if he was agreeing with her or not.

'I'm not hurting you, am I?'

Luis shook his head and shifted a little, the rough towel rubbing beneath his crotch, which was precisely where he did *not* want to focus his attention. *Santo cielos!* No, she was not hurting him—but he wondered if she was trying to torture him. Resting his cheek against his crossed arms, he closed his eyes, unable to decide whether this was heaven or hell. Or perhaps a mixture of both.

What the hell was happening here?

He could feel her hands moving further down his back, skating tantalisingly over the taut lines of his buttocks before alighting on the tops of his thighs. He swallowed as the minutes ticked by and suddenly he found himself lost in the sensations she was producing. If she was nervous, you would never have guessed it. Apart from that nervous flutter of her fingers at the beginning, she had taken to it as if she had been born to stroke at a man's skin like this. Who would ever have thought that his mousey little housekeeper had the touch of an angel?

Yet she had been the model of brisk proficiency from the moment she'd greeted him, with nothing but a brief smile as he had lain face down on the bed. She certainly wasn't flirting with him, which made him wonder what was making him feel so *aroused*. How could Carly—plain little Carly—manage to make him feel like this? Was it because she *wasn't* flirting with him and he wasn't used to that? For a moment he imagined her requesting briskly that he lift up his buttocks, so that she could slide her hands underneath him. He thought about her taking his rapidly growing hardness between her fingers and stroking him to a blessed and swift release.

His mouth dried.

'No, you're not hurting me,' he said eventually, when he was certain his voice wouldn't come out sounding like some kind of strangled groan.

She continued to work in silence. He could feel her fingers sinking deeper into his flesh and as the muscles began to loosen up beneath her touch he couldn't seem to stop himself fantasising about her some more. He wondered what her breasts might look like if she were to remove that hideous overall she was wearing. An image of pale mounds tipped with rosy points swam into his mind with disturbing clarity. He pictured his tongue tracing a slow, wet circle around one puckered nub and he shifted his aroused body again in a vain bid to make himself comfortable.

The movement must have registered, for her hands stilled.

'You're sure I'm not hurting you?'

Against the lavender-scented doughnut of a pillow on which his cheek was resting, Luis shook his head. 'No,' he said huskily. 'You have a very...*natural* touch. I can't believe you haven't done anything like this before.'

'Mary was very helpful. She showed me exactly what to do. She said that if I pressed firmly on key parts of the body...like *this*...that it would be effective. And then last night I studied lots of technique and tips on my computer.'

His instinctive groan of satisfaction made his words come out as a muffled drawl. 'You have nothing better to do on a Friday night than look up massage technique?'

There was a pause.

'I like to do a job properly. And you're paying me a very generous bonus to do this.'

Her emphasis on the financial made him feel

comfortable about interrogating her, although it didn't occur to him until afterwards to wonder why he should be interested in her social life. 'So is there no irritable boyfriend wanting to know why your boss is demanding so much of your time?'

There was another pause, a slightly longer one this time. She seemed to choose her words carefully. 'I don't have a boyfriend, no,' she said. 'But if I did, I don't really think this job would be compatible with it. Not if it was a serious relationship.'

'Why not?'

'Because when you're here the hours are long and erratic and because I'm living in someone else's house and—'

'Not why a live-in job isn't compatible with a relationship,' he interrupted impatiently. 'You wouldn't need to be a genius to work that one out. No, I meant why don't you have a boyfriend?'

Carly rubbed some more oil into the palms of her hands. It was difficult to come up with a reasonable answer to his question. Difficult to come up with anything which sounded sensible when her hands were in contact with his skin like this. If she hadn't been feeling so disorientated by what was happening, she might have told him that her social life was none of his business. Or she might even have hinted that one dreadful experience had put her off men for ever. But she couldn't really think of anything except how gorgeous he felt. She was being bombarded with powerful sensations and none of them were welcome—or expected.

All the blinds had been drawn and the semi-darkened room felt claustrophobic because the dimensions seemed to have shrunk. Candles were wafting out a subtle sandalwood scent and there was faint whale-like music coming from the sound system, just as Mary had suggested. She knew these small additions were intended to create a relaxed atmosphere and maybe it was working for Luis, but it certainly wasn't working for her.

Because the unimaginable was happening. Instead of being frozen with fear, all she could feel was a slow-building pleasure whenever she touched him. She stared down at his olive-skinned body, because where else was she going to look? And even though he was wearing a pair of black briefs instead of those three terrifyingly small towels which had been covering him yesterday, they weren't nearly as much of an advantage as they should have been. Because yes, they provided a necessary barrier of modesty—but they also emphasised the very masculine outlines of his body. They made the rocky globes of his buttocks look as if they'd been coated in liquorice, and liquorice had always been her favourite kind of sweet.

'I'm not really interested in men,' she said at last, her words making a mockery of her thoughts.

'Ah. You prefer women?'

'No!' She was shocked by his openness, and unreasonably hurt by his assumption. She told herself that he was perfectly entitled to think what he liked about her, just as she was perfectly within her rights to tell him that her sexuality was none of his business. But something made her answer him. As if she wanted him to know. *Needed* him to know. 'I'm…straight.'

'Ah.' He turned his head to the side and she could see the faint smile which curved his lips. 'So why is there no man in your life?'

'It drives me mad when people say that. It's the first thing people ask a single woman.' She started massaging again, pressing the heels of her hands hard against the firm flesh, aware that she was running the risk of sounding defensive but suddenly she didn't care. 'You don't have a girlfriend, do you? But I certainly don't make it sound like some kind of character fault, or start interrogating you about it.'

'I don't have one particular partner, no, but I certainly have girlfriends from time to time. You, on the other hand, don't.'

Her hands stopped mid-stroke and she stared at them. She thought they looked like pale starfish in a sea of gold. 'How do you know that, when you're not here most of the time?'

'Because my estate manager keeps me up to speed with what's going on. I like to know what's happening with someone who has the entire run of my house while I'm not here, so obviously I enquire about you from time to time. Not that he tells me anything very interesting since, apparently, you live the life of a nun.'

Carly tensed, hearing the implicit criticism in his tone. 'There's nothing wrong with nuns,' she said.

'I didn't suggest there was. But you haven't taken any vows since you came to work for me, have you, Carly? Certainly not poverty or obedience,' he persisted mockingly.

'Actually, as an employer you do seem to require total obedience from your staff—though I can't deny that you pay very well.'

'Which only leaves chastity,' he said. 'Doesn't it?'

Carly's heart thundered again as she forced herself to restart the massage, trying to concentrate on the slow, circular movements instead of the bizarre turn of their conversation. 'What I do in my spare time is none of your business.'

'He said that you always seem to have your head in a book,' observed Luis, as if she hadn't spoken. 'And that you go to evening classes in the nearby town.'

'And is there something wrong with wanting to improve myself?' she demanded. 'Perhaps I should throw a wild party when you leave. Give the gardeners and the estate manager enough ammunition to earn me a reputation.'

'Why, do you like wild parties?' he challenged.

'No.'

'Me neither,' he said unexpectedly.

'So how does that work?' she asked, with a frown. 'When you throw them on a regular basis. The house is always full of people. Why, you could almost employ a full-time party planner.'

'I agree—they have become something of a habit. A hangover from my racing days when wild parties were *de rigueur,* but recently I have grown bored with them.' His bare shoulders rose in a shrug. 'I find that they are all exactly the same.'

Carly blinked. How peculiar. She'd thought he'd loved the crazy gatherings which all the locals talked about for weeks afterwards. When hordes of the rich and beautiful converged onto his country estate—some of them travelling from as far as Paris and New York. The women were usually the generic blondes he was so fond of, with their tiny dresses and seeking eyes. On more than one occasion, Carly had been standing making pots of coffee at four in the morning, while some poor creature sobbed her eyes out over the kitchen table, because Luis had taken some other woman to bed instead of her. On another memorable occasion, she had opened the door to the drawing room and found a French supermodel lying completely starkers on a fur rug, waiting in vain for Luis and not realising he was already on a plane which was heading for Morocco.

'There.' Carly stopped massaging at last, suddenly aware of the slow trickle of sweat which was sliding in a path between her breasts. Was it the heat which was making them feel so much bigger than usual? Making their tips feel so uncomfortably hard and prickling against her uniform so that she found herself wanting to rub at them. And why was she suddenly looking at the golden gleam of his bare back and thinking it was so physically perfect that it would work as an illustration in the pages of an anatomy book? She swallowed. 'Feeling better?'

'I'm feeling...good,' he said indistinctly.

Hastily, Carly wiped her hands on a towel. She had to stop thinking like this. She had to start regarding him with the impartiality she'd always had before now. 'I think that's enough for now, don't you?' She kept her voice brisk. 'We can have another session before...er, before you retire for the night. You can get up if you like, Luis.'

But Luis didn't want to get up. Or rather, he didn't feel capable of getting up, not in the way that she meant and not without making it very clear that he was having very erotic feelings about her. He could feel the hard throb at his groin and the sharp aching in his balls and found himself in the unthinkable position of being aroused—*by Miss Mouse.* And he still wasn't sure how that had happened. Surely it couldn't just be because she was *touching* him, because if that was the case then he would have felt something more potent than irritation towards Mary—the physiotherapist he had just sacked.

The aching intensified, but his impatient squirm only made the hardness worse, instead of relieving it. He scowled into the stupid scented doughnut of a pillow. Weeks of doing nothing had driven him close to crazy with no work, no play and no sex. Worse still, his confinement had left him with time to think and he was a man who preferred to *do*. Stripped of his constant need for action, he was forced into the unwanted position of introspection.

His incarceration in hospital had made him stop and take a look at his life and realise what a circus it had become. He'd thought about his different homes dotted around the world and the swollen entourage who accompanied him everywhere, and it had been like looking at the world of someone he didn't know. When had he managed to acquire so many hangers-on? He remembered their barely disguised shock when he had sent them to his main base in Buenos Aires, with Diego at the helm. And the strange calm which had descended on the house once they'd gone, leaving him alone with his mousey housekeeper.

He shifted his thigh a fraction as he thought how efficiently Carly had slotted into her new role as temporary masseuse. It seemed she was as proficient at rehabilitation as she was at running his house for him. Minutes before his massage, she had overseen the daily ballet exercises intended to strengthen his damaged pelvis. She hadn't made any predictable jokes about men doing ballet, but had simply stood beside him, counting the small elevations of his legs, with a look of fierce determination on her face.

'How about a swim now, Luis?'

Her soft voice ruptured his disturbing thoughts and it was with a sense of relief that he realised that his erection had subsided.

He yawned. 'Is that a suggestion?'

'No, it's an order—since you seem to respond much better to those.' She pulled up the blind and peered outside. 'Oh, dear, it's raining again.'

'It's always raining in this damned country.'

'That's what makes the fields so green,' she said sweetly. 'Never mind. At least we can use the indoor pool.'

'But I don't like the indoor pool,' he growled. 'You know that. It's claustrophobic.'

'And this room isn't?'

'I'm not planning to swim in here,' he snapped. 'So why don't we just go outside and use the big pool? Live dangerously for once.'

Carly turned back from the window, her mouth flattening with a disapproval she couldn't quite hide as she looked at him. She knew that was the kind of crazy thing he did. She'd witnessed people diving into his rain-lashed swimming pool, fully clothed, and she'd come down early the next morning to find glasses full of rain and champagne. Once she had even found a pair of knickers hanging from one of the flagpoles and one of the gardeners had been forced to shin up and get them back down again. What must it be like to live a life as decadent as his? she wondered.

'Because I don't like to live dangerously,' she said repressively. 'And perhaps if you didn't, then you wouldn't have ended up occupying a hospital bed for so long and probably blocking it for someone who really needs it. As it happens, the grass is absolutely sodden and the tiles around the swimming pool will be wet and slippery.'

'Sca—*ry*,' he said sarcastically.

She didn't react to his taunt, even though he seemed to be spoiling for *some* kind of fight. What was the matter with him today? He was even more bad-tempered than usual—and that was saying something. She set her lips into a disapproving line. 'So unless you want to risk falling over and complicating your recovery, then I'd advise playing safe and using the indoor pool, which was designed with rainy days like these in mind.'

'Don't you ever get tired of being the sensible voice of reason?'

And don't you ever get tired of being the perennial bad-boy playboy? It was only with difficulty that she stopped herself from saying it out loud as she turned to face him. 'I thought that's what you were paying me for.'

'That, and your cooking.' He paused, his thick black lashes half veiling his eyes. 'So you don't like living dangerously?'

Emphatically, Carly shook her head. No, she certainly did not. On the contrary, she had always wanted to live safe. She had craved a security and stability which had always eluded her. But Luis didn't really want to know that, did he? He was asking the question in that throwaway way he sometimes did, like an owner throwing his dog a scrap of food from the table. He wasn't interested in her as a person; she was just a tiny cog in the giant wheel designed to keep his life running smoothly. 'Not really,' she said. 'You do enough danger for both of us.'

He gave an exaggerated sigh. 'Okay, Miss Sensible—you win. The indoor pool it is. Go and find your swimsuit and meet me in there.'

But his mocking was ringing around her head as Carly ran upstairs to change into her costume, because he had touched a nerve. Being sensible wasn't something most people aspired to but she'd always been that way. At school she had been the reliable first choice if you needed someone to help with your science homework, or to spend a whole playtime looking for a lost charm from somebody's bracelet. *Careful Carly*, they had called her and as a nickname she hadn't particularly liked it. It wasn't cool to be careful—it was just the way she'd been made.

She reached her room at the top of the house and shut the door behind her, leaning against it to get her breath back. The attic space was large, with sloping ceilings and a dramatic view over the gardens and the fields beyond. Up here she was among the treetops. Up here you could see the most amazing sunrises and sunsets, which filled the room with a rich red light. There was a little desk, on which she did her studying, and on the wall above the small fireplace hung the little watercolour her father had painted, the year before he'd become too ill to hold a brush any more.

Sliding open one of the drawers, she fished around and found her swimming costume, knowing that the last thing she wanted was for Luis to see her in it. She was too fleshy. Too pale. Too everything. And although she knew that comparison was pointless, she couldn't help thinking about the women who usually shared the pool with him. Leggy supermodels, wearing tiny bits of string which they called bikinis. She shivered as she stripped out of her bra and pants, her skin cold and resistant as she tugged on the one-piece. She thought how faded it looked and how, rather alarmingly, it seemed to have shrunk.

The rain was bashing hard against the window and some of the showier plants in the flower beds had been flattened to the ground. The dark blue petals of the delphiniums lay scattered on the sodden earth, as if some exotic bird had recently had its feathers plucked. Carly found herself remembering that expression her mother used to say: *Fine feathers make a fine bird.*

But now wasn't a good time to remind herself why her doll-like sister had always been given the cream of the crop, while she had been dressed in more practical outfits. After all, why would ungainly Carly be given the delicate clothes favoured by a thespian mother, desperate to create a mini-me image of herself?

When she'd been old enough to buy her own clothes, she had become more adventurous, until that disastrous night which had ended up with her at first wanting to die and then to just fade into the background. And she had become very good at doing that.

She thought about the questions Luis had asked her. Intrusive questions about her sex life or, rather, the lack of it. For a moment she forgot the indignation that her employer should be arrogant enough to question her about something like that. Suddenly she got a glimpse of her life as others must see it. As someone who never went out and never had boyfriends. Who lived in the billionaire's house and polished and cleaned it even when he wasn't there. As someone who lived in a staid little world which kept her safe, but which now seemed to mock her.

And Luis didn't know about her ambitions, did he? He didn't realise that behind her dull image was someone who was going to do good some day. Someone who could hopefully use the brain she'd been given and not have to rely on her looks to better herself.

Pulling on a towelling robe, she hurried down to the pool to find Luis waiting for her and she couldn't help the instinctive shiver which ran down her spine. Silhouetted against the enormous curved window which overlooked the woods, he was wearing nothing but a moulded pair of swim-shorts and, from where she stood, Carly thought he looked almost completely fit again.

Despite the severity of his injuries, he had certainly regained his physical strength very quickly—probably because he had been at the peak of fitness before the accident. His dark body still looked immensely tough, despite the crutches he was leaning on. Wavy black tendrils of hair kissed the base of his neck and he seemed lost in thought as he stared out at the Indian Leaf trees whose summer blossoms were creamy-white against the greyness of the day.

He turned as she walked in, and something very peculiar happened to her as their eyes met across the turquoise pool. It was like the disorientation she'd felt when she'd massaged him earlier, only it was worse. Much worse. She stared at him across the echoing space and there was no sound other than the quiet lapping of water and the unnaturally loud pounding of her heart. She could feel her breath drying in her throat and suddenly her chest was tight and she was having trouble breathing. It was happening again and she didn't want it to happen. She didn't want to look at a man like Luis and *desire* him. She didn't want to feel this hot little ache at the pit of her belly or the sudden warmth which had started flushing over her skin. Why him, and why *now*?

Was it because she had touched him in an intimate way and broken a taboo which had haunted her for such a long time? She had run her fingers over his almost naked body and had been able to do so because everyone knew that the massage was a kind of *healing*.

But maybe she had been wrong. Maybe it had been more than that. What if that touch had woken something she'd thought was dead, but which had been lying dormant all this time? Something which was now assuming a life of its own and making her look at him with a terrible and tearing kind of *hunger*.

She blinked, wanting to clear her vision and make everything go back to how it had been before. She wanted to go back to thinking of Luis as a generous but extremely arrogant boss. She wanted to be troubled by nothing more onerous than trying to get her head round the book on quantum physics she was currently reading. Because she didn't *do* desire and all the dark stuff which came with it. Wasn't she a total failure in that department? *Hadn't she been told that in no uncertain terms?*

She saw him glance across as she slipped off her robe and that glance, more than anything, killed off some of the feelings which had been multiplying like bacteria inside her. Was that *disbelief* she could read in his eyes? Of course it was. He'd probably never seen a woman who wasn't a size zero. Looking at her curvy body, he might think that she usually finished up all the *alfajores* once he'd flown back to wherever was next on his exotic list of destinations. And he would be right.

Forcing a quick, professional smile, she walked towards him. 'Ready?' she questioned.

'I've been ready for quite some time,' he said acidly. 'But, as usual, you were late.'

'It took me a while to find my costume.'

'Sorry for the inconvenience,' he said sarcastically. 'Perhaps I should have given you more warning. Written it down in triplicate and signed it first.'

She decided not to react. To just pretend that nothing was the matter, but it wasn't easy when she was being confronted by a bare and powerful torso which was making her want to squirm with embarrassment. 'Anyway, we're here now,' she said brightly. 'Just make sure you go backwards down the ladder.'

'I think I know how to get into the damned swimming pool by now.'

Carefully, she took the crutches from him and propped them up against the wall. 'I was only trying to—'

'Well, stop trying,' he snapped. 'I'm fed up with people *trying*. I've been doing this damned regime for weeks and I think I've just about managed to get my head round it. Next thing you'll be teaching me how to cut up my meat using a knife and fork. Or maybe even start spoon-feeding me.'

For Carly, it was the final straw. Coming on top of the insecurity she was feeling at having to stand in front of him, shivering half to death in an unflattering swimsuit, and the fact that she had been shoehorned into a role she didn't want, something inside her flipped. She turned and glared at him. 'Do you have to be *quite* so bad-tempered, when I'm only trying to help you?'

There was a pause as their eyes clashed in a fierce and silent battle. She felt herself tense to find herself caught in that intense black spotlight and she wondered what snapped insult he was about to come out with next. And then, unexpectedly, he sighed.

'I know you are,' he said. 'It's only frustration which is making me so unbearable. The aftermath of this damned accident has gone on for weeks and sometimes it feels as if it's never going to end.'

'Yes.' She chewed on her bottom lip. 'I suppose that's one way of looking at it.'

He raised his brows. 'Unless you're about to tell me that I am pretty unbearable generally?'

Quickly, she glanced down at his bare feet, thinking how pale and perfect his toenails looked against the dark olive of his skin. 'That isn't for me to say.'

'No instant denial, then, Carly?' he mocked. 'Leading me to conclude that I *am* unbearable?'

She lifted her head then and met the mocking challenge in his eyes. 'You aren't exactly known for your sweet and even temper,' she said, and to her surprise he actually laughed as he lowered his powerful body into the pool.

'No, I suppose I'm not. Come on, Carly—aren't you coming in?' he questioned, hitting the surface of the water with the flat of his hand so that an iridescent little plume of spray went showering upwards and fell in tiny droplets which gleamed against his dark skin. 'Mary always did.'

I'll bet she did, thought Carly as she slipped into the water beside him. Yet wasn't *she* doing exactly what Mary had been guilty of doing? She was having some *very* inappropriate thoughts about her boss, only she was also being a bit of a hypocrite, because hadn't she disapproved of the physiotherapist's behaviour?

She waded further into the water and shivered as the cool water reached her tummy. Goosebumps iced over her skin and she felt the tips of her breasts hardening again, just as they'd done earlier.

In an attempt to conceal it, she leaned back against the tiled wall and splashed water over her arms. 'You're supposed to do ten lengths.'

'I know I am, but I'm planning to do twenty.'

'Do you think that's wise?'

He gave her a hard smile. 'Let's find out, shall we?'

She watched as he struck out, making no concessions towards his injuries as he cleaved through the water like a golden-dark arrow. He swam with the same energy and determination which he applied to everything in life, but after twelve lengths she could see that he had grown pale and his mouth was tight with tension.

'Stop now,' she said, as he came up for air, his black hair plastered to his head like a seal. 'For heaven's sake—slow down, Luis. You're not in some kind of race.'

But he was stubborn, of course he was, and for him life *was* a race. She wasn't surprised when he shook his head and continued but when he'd finished, he was exhausted. Hauling his body out of the water, he propped his elbows onto the edge of the pool and rested his head on them, saying nothing until he had regained his breath.

At last he looked up at her, his eyes gleaming blackly from between wet, matted lashes. 'How was that?'

'You know exactly how it was. You did twenty lengths—double that recommended by the physiotherapist. You want praise for disobeying her instructions?'

'*Sí.* I demand praise. Heaps of it piled high onto my head. So why don't you wipe that disapproving look off your face for once, and tell me how good I am?' His mouth curved into a provocative smile. 'You know you want to.'

Carly stiffened as something unfamiliar prickled over her skin. Was he *flirting* with her? She stared at him, her eyes blinking. Surely not. Unless flirting was almost like a reflex action for him, a bit like a goldfish gasping for air if somebody tipped its bowl onto the floor. *It's just sweet-talk and it doesn't mean anything,* she told herself fiercely. *So don't act as if it does.* 'You probably overextended yourself, but, yes, you were good,' she agreed grudgingly. 'Actually, you were very good.'

He raised his wet eyebrows. 'Why, Carly,' he murmured. 'Praise from you is praise indeed.'

Flustered now, she tried not to let it show, dipping down below the surface of the water, mainly to try to distract herself again. But when she stood up again she could see that Luis's eyes had narrowed and it took a moment for her to realise that he was staring at her with fascination. Or, more specifically, he was staring at her breasts.

The stretchy fabric of her modest one-piece had suddenly become tight and shiny and was clinging to her like a second skin. Embarrassingly, she could feel her nipples pushing against the wet fabric like two little bullets.

Had he noticed that?

Oh, God. What if he had?

'I think you ought to get out now,' she said quickly. 'Before you get too cold.'

'Or too hot,' he amended, but his words were so indistinct that she told herself she must have misheard them. She *must* have done. Unless she was seriously imagining that Luis Martinez—one of the world's greatest lovers—was making a suggestive remark to *her*.

'Let's go,' she said, and dived beneath the water to escape his watchful black eyes.

She swam further than she had intended but she needn't have bothered, because the cold water failed to have the effect it should have done. And when she rose to the surface, gasping for breath, she still had that same terrible aching in her breasts when she looked at him.

CHAPTER THREE

IN A STREAM of impatient Spanish, Luis cursed loudly and eloquently. Outside, the wind howled and rain battered remorselessly against the tall windows. Never-ending rivulets slid down the glass as the sound of the summer storm served as background noise in the scarlet and gold drawing room.

When was this damned rain ever going to stop?

Redirecting his gaze to the table at the far side of the room, he watched as Carly bent over a tray and poured him a tiny cup of espresso.

He felt another unwelcome jerk of desire, jackknifed through his groin with an exquisite precision which made him want to squirm. He scowled instead.

He was bored.

Bored and frustrated.

And one must be as a direct result of the other, he reasoned. Because why else would he be feeling such powerful pangs of lust for someone like little Miss Mouse?

Unobserved, he let his eyes drift over her, trying to work it out. For once, the shapeless cut of her jeans managed to enhance her figure, though not through any deliberate intention on her part. When she bent over like that, the denim stretched tightly over her bottom and emphasised the generous curves of her derriere. She ought to wear close-fitting clothes more often, he thought hungrily. Just as he ought to be in his study analysing the stock market, or reading through the stack of emails which Diego had sent through to him earlier. His mouth tightened and the need to distract himself from her luscious body became paramount.

'Play cards with me, Carly,' he said suddenly.

She turned round to look at him, her expression at first startled, then decidedly wary.

'I don't play cards,' she said.

'Then I'll teach you.'

Still she hesitated.

'What's the matter?' he drawled. 'Afraid I'll corrupt you? One game of poker and you'll be gambling away all your hard-earned wages?'

Wishing that he would stop looking at her like that, Carly straightened up and carried his coffee across the room, putting it down on the table beside him.

Corrupt her? She wondered if he had any idea what a good job he'd already done in that department. Wouldn't he be appalled if he knew how much he was on her mind these days? If he realised that she lay in bed thinking about him at night, when the silence and the darkness of her room seemed to magnify her thoughts. Thoughts which felt like longing, but which were closely followed by terrifying memories. Yet even those memories weren't enough to prevent the tingling in her breasts, or the molten ache low in her belly as she lay beneath the feather-soft duvet.

She had felt...*frustrated*...but had found herself recoiling from needs which she had re-pressed for so long. She kept telling herself that all she needed was to maintain some kind of balance, until things got back to normal again.

But when would that be?

When her boss was well enough to go back to Buenos Aires, or New York, or France or wherever he was planning to take up residence next? When he put some natural distance be-tween them, so that all these stupid feelings would fade away? When she could go back to the quiet, studious life she had forged for her-self here and put him out of her mind.

And sitting playing card games wasn't going to help, was it? Not on top of all the increasingly intimate massage sessions and those long and distracting sessions in the pool. She needed to spend less time with him, not more.

'I don't think we have any cards,' she said.

'Yes, we do. In my bedroom,' he said. 'In the desk. Second drawer, on the left. Go and get them, will you, Carly?'

She raised her eyebrows.

He sighed. 'Please.'

'What if I told you that I don't particularly want to play cards.'

'Then I might be forced to pull rank.'

'So it's an order?'

He slanted her an arrogant smile. 'Most definitely it is.'

Carly turned and left the room without another word but her footsteps felt heavy as she mounted the stairs. She felt trapped—like a fly caught in the sticky temptation of a spider's web. The weather had effectively kept them prisoners in this big house so that sometimes it felt as if they were the only two people in the world. And meanwhile, her dilemma was compounded by her growing feelings for him. Because even she recognised that something had changed.

In the past she had thought of him as a distant and demanding figure, but hadn't that been preferable to *this*? To finding that she was actually enjoying his company in a perverse sort of way. Just her and him and the worst summer rains the country had known for a decade. Cooped up and going stir-crazy, with the lanes around the estate thick with mud and puddles. Luis couldn't drive and he didn't want to take the train to London. And he told her that he didn't want people coming over, drinking his wine and eating his food, and taunting him with all the things he found himself unable to do.

The most disturbing thing of all was that Carly was discovering how much she *liked* having him all to herself.

Pushing open the door to his bedroom, she entered the oak-panelled suite which took up almost all the first floor of the stately home. She'd been up here earlier, making his bed as she always did, changing his expensive Egyptian sheets, which were inevitably tangled— even when he slept alone.

Walking over to his desk, she found her gaze drawn to the two photos standing at either end of the gleaming surface. One was of his mother with her sad eyes and raven hair and the other an iconic shot of Luis, taken the first time he'd become world champion. His hair was wet with the spray of champagne and he was holding a massive silver trophy aloft.

It was funny, she'd seen these photos countless times and most days she dusted around their heavy silver frames without really noticing them. But today she felt like an intruder snooping around. As if her role in this house had subtly changed and she wasn't sure how to deal with it.

'Carly!'

Luis's impatient voice rang through the house, and quickly she found the pack of cards and ran back downstairs to find him sitting where she'd left him.

He glared at her. 'What kept you?'

'I didn't realise I was being timed. I was just daydreaming.'

'And what were you daydreaming about?' he questioned silkily.

She could feel the hot lick of colour to her cheeks, terrified he might guess. 'Nothing,' she said quickly and walked over to the card table.

Wincing a little, Luis levered himself to his feet before joining her and, for some reason, he became aware of the lamplight making intriguing shadows on her rather square face. He noticed the way her breasts moved as she fidgeted with the cards. And he wondered what she'd say if she knew that he'd been sitting here wondering what she would look like naked. He pulled out a chair and sat down, wondering how long this madness was going to continue, and his mouth hardened. Because he had never slept with anyone on his payroll—and he didn't intend to start, not with Carly.

He held out his hand for the pack.

'So what are we going to play?' she questioned.

It was unfortunate that her innocent question only fuelled his frustration, and suddenly all he could think about was the brush of her skin against his as he took the cards from her and he wanted more of it. He wanted to play a game which had nothing to do with hearts or clubs or diamonds. He wanted to play a very grown-up game which involved baring those intriguing curves and feasting his mouth and his hands on them, until he had sated his inconvenient hunger.

He shook his head, trying to clear the powerful images from his mind. 'Do you want to try learning poker?' he asked.

'Is it easy?'

'Not really.'

'In that case, I'd love to.'

He raised his eyebrows. 'Don't say I didn't warn you.'

He shuffled the cards and dealt them and watched her brow pleating in concentration as he explained the rules to her. To his surprise he didn't have to repeat them and she seemed to grasp the concept of the game with remarkable speed.

He had expected—what? That he'd beat her without trying and soon become bored with effortless victory as had happened so often in the past? He was midway through the second game when he realised she was good. Actually, she was very good. And he was having to keep all his wits about him to compete against a mind which was more agile than he'd given her credit for.

She was bright, he thought in confusion. She was very bright.

'Are you sure you haven't played this before?' he questioned suspiciously.

'If I'd played before, then why would I have allowed you to explain all the rules to me?'

'Gamesmanship?'

'That's a very cynical viewpoint, Luis,' she said as she studied the fanned-out cards in her hand.

'Maybe life has made me cynical.'

She looked up and extended her bottom lip in an exaggerated pout. 'Oh, poor diddums!'

It wasn't an expression he knew but the meaning was clear and Luis found himself laughing in response. But that confused him even more, because women didn't usually amuse him, unless it was with the light, teasing comments they sometimes made when they were removing their clothes. Women had their place, but humour rarely featured in it. And suddenly he found himself intrigued by this badly dressed woman with her surprisingly street-sharp grasp of the complex card game. 'You do realise,' he said slowly, 'that I know practically nothing about you.'

She looked up and the light from the lamp shone directly into her face, turning her eyes the colour of clear, bright honey. And Luis suddenly found himself thinking: *They are beautiful eyes.*

'Why should you?' she questioned. 'It isn't relevant to my work. You don't need to know anything about me.'

'A woman who deflects questions about herself?' he drawled. 'Can this really be happening, or am I dreaming?'

'That's an outrageous generalisation to make about women.'

'And one which happens to be true. Generalisations usually are.' He leaned back against the chair and narrowed his eyes. 'So how long have you worked for me now? It must be a year?'

'It's two and a half, actually.'

'That long?'

'Time flies when you're having fun,' she said.

He heard the flippant note in her voice as he continued to study her. 'Being a housekeeper is an unusual job for a woman your age, isn't it?' he observed slowly.

'I suppose so.' She shrugged. 'But it's a good job if you don't have any qualifications. Or if you need somewhere to live,' she added, almost as an afterthought.

He put his cards face down on the table. 'You don't have any qualifications? That surprises me. You are clearly bright enough—judging by the way you've just picked up a relatively complicated card game.'

Carly didn't answer straight away and not just because his words sounded so patronising. She didn't want to tell him about her hopes and dreams—she didn't want to *expose* herself in any way to him because she sensed a certain *danger* in doing that. If it had been any other time, she might have distracted herself with a task which needed doing and hoped he'd forget about it. But it wasn't any other time—it was now—and she was out of her usual comfort zone. She couldn't pretend that she needed to go and see to something in the kitchen because she suspected he would overrule her. Luis wanted to talk and Luis was paying her wages. And what Luis wanted, he generally got.

'I've been trying to make up for lost time,' she said. 'Which is why I did those evening classes. And why I've taken a couple of the science exams I really ought to have taken at school.'

'You've been studying *science*?'

She heard the surprise in his voice. 'Yes. What's the matter with that? Some people do actually *like* those subjects.'

'But they're not usually women.'

'Again, another outrageous generalisation.' She shook her head in mock despair. 'That's the second sexist thing you've said within the space of two minutes, Luis.'

'How can it be sexist if it's true? Look at the stats if you don't believe me. Men dominate the field of science. And maths,' he added.

'Which might have a lot more to do with teaching methods and expectations than because they have scientifically superior brains.'

His eyes glittered. 'I think we'll have to differ on that.'

Carly could feel herself getting hot as he ran a speculative gaze over her and once again she was aware of that whispering feeling of danger. 'As you wish,' she said, wanting to change the subject and talk about something else, but it seemed he was having none of it.

'Which science were you good at?' he persisted.

'All of them. Biology and chemistry. Maths, too. I loved them all.'

'So why—?'

'Did I flunk my exams?' She abandoned all pretence of playing the game and put her own cards down on the table. She didn't want to answer this, but she knew Luis well enough to recognise that he wouldn't let up. And pain grew less over time, didn't it? As the years went by you could talk about things which had happened and make them sound almost *conversational*. 'Because my father was…well, he was very ill when I was younger and as a consequence I missed out on quite a bit of school work.'

'I'm sorry,' he said, and Carly almost wished he hadn't because it was harder to keep things in perspective when his voice had softened like that.

'Oh, these things happen,' she said.

'What exactly happened?' he probed, his dark eyes narrowed. 'What aren't you telling me, Carly? People have sick parents but still manage to pass exams.'

His persistence was as difficult to ignore as it was surprising, since he wasn't known for taking an interest in the personal life of his staff. And suddenly Carly found herself telling him. It was, she realised, a long time since she'd told anyone because people didn't want to hear hard-luck stories, did they? It was the modern trend to portray your life as if it were just one long, happy party; to act as if you were having fun all the time.

'It was one of those long-term chronic things,' she said, her voice growing quieter. 'He couldn't get out of the house much, so I used to come home from school, and sit and tell him about my day. Sometimes I'd read to him—he liked that. Then by the time I'd cooked supper and the nurse had come in to put him to bed, I'd be too tired to do my homework. Or maybe I was just too lazy,' she added, her attempt to lighten the mood failing spectacularly, for not a flicker of a smile had touched his suddenly sombre face.

'And did he recover?'

His voice was still doing that dangerous thing. That soft thing which was making her feel things she had no right to feel—certainly not about him. It was making her feel *vulnerable,* and she'd spent a lifetime trying not to feel like that. Carly pressed her lips together. She never cried about it these days, but the mind could still play funny tricks on you, couldn't it? Sometimes an innocent question could make your eyes well up without warning and she didn't want that happening now. Not in front of her boss. She shook her head. 'No. I'm afraid he didn't. He died when I was nineteen.'

His ebony gaze seemed to pierce right through her skin.

'And what about your mother?' he questioned. 'Wasn't she around to help?'

This bit was more difficult. It was hard to convey what had happened without making Mum sound like some kind of wicked witch, which she wasn't—she was just someone who could occasionally be a bit misguided.

'She wasn't very...*good* with illness. Some people aren't,' said Carly, injecting that breezy note into her voice which she'd mastered so well. The one which implied that she totally supported her mother's decision to live out her own failed dreams through her beautiful, younger daughter. She remembered the way her mum used to talk about Bella making it big through modelling, but saying that you needed to pump money in to get money out. And that had been what had driven her. What had made her bleed their dwindling bank account dry—a big gamble which had ultimately failed. And even if it had succeeded—so what? As if material success could ever cancel out all the sadness which had been playing out at home. 'My mother was busy helping my sister launch her career. She's a model,' she added.

'Oh?' Luis's eyebrows rose. 'That's a term which usually covers a multitude of sins. Would I have heard of her?'

'You might have done,' said Carly. 'Though maybe not yet. She does lots of catalogue work. And last year she was hired for the opening of a new shopping complex in Dubai.'

'I see.'

Carly heard the trace of sarcasm in his voice and she bristled. Because that was the thing about families, wasn't it? You could criticise your own until the cows came home, but woe betide anyone else who attempted to do the same.

'She's doing a lot of swimwear shoots at the moment and lingerie modelling. She's *very* beautiful.'

'Is she?'

Carly could hear the doubt in his voice and all her own insecurities came rushing in to swamp her, like dark strands of seaweed pulling her down into the water so that she couldn't breathe. Did he think that someone like her was incapable of having a beautiful sister, with hair like white gold and naturally plump lips, which made you think she'd had Botox? A sister whose ankles and wrists were so delicate that sometimes you worried that they might snap, like spun sugar. Because Bella was all those things—and more.

And didn't she *have* to believe that her sister would one day achieve the success which she and her mother had yearned for? Otherwise it would make all those years of sacrifice and heartbreak count for nothing. It would make the memory of her father's reedy voice as he'd called in vain for his wife all the harder to bear. It would make the debts and the loss of their house seem a complete waste. And it would stop Carly from shrugging and accepting fate the way she'd learned to. Because the last thing she wanted was to feel bitter, when she remembered screwing up her application form for medical school into a tight little ball and hurling it onto the fire.

'Yes,' she said fiercely. 'She's the most exquisite woman you could ever wish to meet.'

For a moment, Luis didn't say anything. He thought her mother sounded shallow and uncaring, but he wasn't particularly shocked by that. She was a woman, wasn't she? And he had yet to meet a single one who could be trusted.

But it must have been hard on Miss Mouse. Even if she was trying to make it sound as if she was okay with it, he could see her struggling to contain her emotions. And for once he felt a certain empathy with her, even though dealing with a woman's emotions was something he tended to steer clear of. Because this was different. This wasn't someone who was breaking her heart just because she'd put on a couple of kilos, or because a man refused to buy her a diamond ring.

Instead, he saw a bright girl who was good at science, who had flunked her exams because she'd been busy caring for her father. But he wondered who had been looking out for her.

He remembered flitting in and out of consciousness after his recent operation, wondering who had been stroking his brow during the surreal night which had followed. The woman with the soft voice which had washed over him like a cool balm. Next day he'd asked the nurse if he had been hallucinating and she'd told him it had been the girl with the ponytail, in the old raincoat. He remembered frowning and wondering who she was talking about. A kind girl, the nurse had added, and that was when he'd realised that she'd meant Carly.

She had visited him a few times after that and in a strange way he had found himself looking forward to her visits—mainly because she always seemed able to plump up the pillows and make him feel even more comfortable than the nurses. She'd sat beside him rather primly and had suggested he breathe deeply and move his ankles around. Actually, in a quiet way she had been a bit of a *tyrant*, but he seemed to have responded well to her general bossiness. And then one day she'd just stopped coming, and that had been that.

He picked up his coffee and sipped it. Despite her occasional bursts of fierceness, her company had been surprisingly tolerable since they'd been alone in the house, even if she did insist on scurrying away to her room at every available opportunity. Even if she seemed to play down every womanly trait she possessed...

At least tonight she wasn't wearing that ugly uniform she always insisted on, though she had chosen a cotton shirt in yet another forgettable shade of beige. It was not a colour palette he would have ever chosen for her. With those eyes the colour of iced tea he might have dressed her in flame—or maybe scarlet. He gave the glimmer of a smile. Even if she was the antithesis of a scarlet woman.

His gaze flickered to her hands. Working hands, with short, unpainted nails which matched her scrubbed face and no-nonsense hairstyle. Briefly, he wondered why she was content to sublimate her femininity like this. Was it because she had stood for too long in the shadow of her beautiful sister? Or just that caring for her father during her formative years had blotted out her more frivolous side?

He thought that her childhood sounded pretty grim. Or maybe it was that all families were essentially dysfunctional. The wounds they inflicted never really healed, did they? He thought of his own family as the rain began to batter against the window again.

'This weather is crazy,' he said, his voice growing hard with frustration.

'Of course it is. We're in England.'

'But we don't have to be.' He put his cup down

with a rattle and stared at her. 'Do you have a passport?'

'Of course I do.'

'Good.' He picked up his cards again. 'Then make sure you're ready to leave first thing to-morrow morning.'

'Leave?' Carly blinked. 'Leave for where?'

'St Jean Cap Ferrat. I have a house there.'

'You mean...' She looked at him in confusion. 'Cap Ferrat in the south of France?'

He raised his eyebrows. 'Is there any other?'

'But why do you want to go there, and why so suddenly?'

'Because I'm bored,' he said silkily.

Carly looked at him uneasily. She'd heard enough stories about his Mediterranean villa to know what it was like. It was where the beautiful people hung out. Where someone like her would never fit in. 'I...I think I'd prefer to stay here, if that's okay with you.'

'But it is not *okay* with me,' he returned, his voice edged with a steely arrogance which cut through her like a blade. 'You are being paid an enormous amount of money to make my life easier, Carly, which means doing as *I* wish. And number one on my wish list is to get out of this damned rain and feel a little warmth on my skin again. So why don't you wipe that dazed look off your face and start packing?'

CHAPTER FOUR

HATEFUL, ARROGANT MAN.

Even the beauty of her surroundings couldn't blot out Carly's indignation at the way Luis had spoken to her just before they'd left England.

You are being paid an enormous amount of money.

Yes, she knew that.

To make my life easier.

She knew that, too. So did that give him the right to treat her like a portable piece of property who could just be shifted around when it suited him? Her mouth tightened. But what Luis wanted, Luis got, didn't he? And if the South American billionaire decided to uproot to his villa in the south of France because he was *bored* and wanted to feel the heat of the sun on his body, then that was exactly what would happen.

But Carly forced herself to stay positive as she packed her suitcase, concentrating instead on the massive bonus he was paying her. It made her dream of getting to med school one step closer. It was so close now that she could almost *taste* it. All she had to do was tolerate the arrogant Argentinian playboy for a little while longer and then she would be free.

They had spent a surreal morning getting here, boarding a private jet, which had flown them from London to Nice, where they'd been spotted by a lone paparazzi who apparently spent his days waiting for famous passengers to arrive on the incoming flights. Carly watched as he leapt in front of them, shooting off a role of film as Luis walked through the airport terminal.

He wasn't striding at his usual powerful pace, but his walking stick didn't seem to deter the attentions of a group of women who converged on him, looking like beautiful clones with their sun-kissed hair and frayed denim shorts. Instantly, they began to thrust pieces of paper in front of his face.

'Sign for me, Luis?'

'Want to come to a party later, Luis?' asked one, boldly trying to shove a card into the top pocket of his denim shirt.

But despite his waving them away with an impatient hand, the girls simply took out their camera phones and started clicking frantically instead.

'Does that happen very often?' asked Carly as they climbed into the powerful car which was waiting for them outside the terminal.

'Walking through an arrivals lounge when you get off a plane?'

'There's no need for sarcasm,' she said tightly. 'I meant, that kind of fan girl attention.'

He shrugged. 'Everywhere I go.'

'And does it get too much?'

He shot her a sardonic look. 'What do you think?'

She hesitated. 'I think that your life is...

strange. That it manages to be both very public and very isolated at the same time.'

'Ten out of ten for perception,' he said mockingly.

She clipped her seat belt closed as the car began to pull away. 'Yet you didn't take any of those women up on their offers,' she observed, 'when many men in your position might have done.'

He gave a short laugh. 'You don't think that I've grown jaded with that kind of liaison? That those kinds of women are as interchangeable as the tyres I used to get through during a race?'

'That's a mean thing to say.'

'But it's true.'

The words came out more hotly than she had intended. 'Funny how it's never stopped you before.'

'Why would it stop me?' He raised his eyebrows. 'If a man is thirsty, he would be a fool not to drink. You think I should turn down some beautiful, beddable blonde because we have nothing in common other than the fact that our raging hormones seem hell-bent on collision?'

Carly shook her head. 'You are outrageous.'

His lips curved into a smile and his dark eyes gleamed. 'But you knew that already, Carly— I'm just answering your questions as honestly as I know how.'

Yes, he was, thought Carly. And didn't she *admire* his honesty, even if it made her feel uncomfortable at times? He wasn't pretending to be someone he wasn't, was he? Maybe the emptiness in his eyes was an inevitable consequence of having your appetite jaded by being offered too much, too young.

'So do you *like* being famous?' she asked suddenly.

'You make it sound as if I had choice in the matter, but I didn't.' He rested his palms on his denim-covered thighs and flexed his fingers. 'I didn't seek fame. All I wanted was to race and to be the best in the world— the acclamation was just an inevitable spin-off of that.'

But as he met her amber eyes he remembered

that there had been other spin-offs, too. Success on the scale he'd known meant that you could write your own rules as you went along and he'd done exactly that, hadn't he? Big time. He had turned his back on responsibility. He had taken from women but had never given anything back. He hadn't needed to. He had known unbelievable wealth and adulation but nothing had ever filled the dark space deep inside him. Maybe that was the price you paid for fame.

'Maybe I shouldn't have taken on as much advertising as I did,' he said slowly. 'But I was young and the success went to my head and it seemed crazy to turn down that kind of money. And my sponsors were keen for me to do it. Actually, that's an understatement. They wanted someone to sex up the sport as much as possible and I was considered perfect for the role.'

And motor-racing was as sexy as it got, Carly realised. Even she could see that. All that power and testosterone and money—and Luis had exemplified it all with those show-stopping good looks and hard, sexy body. No wonder beautiful strangers thrust their phone numbers at him at airports with innuendo in their voices and hunger in their eyes. No wonder that even women like her weren't immune to his charm.

'And once you're famous, you can't undo it,' she said slowly. 'You can't go back to the person you were before.'

'No. You can't. The world has an image of you and there isn't a thing you can do to change it.'

'Well, that's not quite true. You could…' The words were out before she had time to think about them.

He raised his eyebrows. 'Could what?'

'Nothing.'

'Tell me. I'm interested.'

She shrugged. 'You kind of *bring* publicity on yourself by dating the sort of women who give tell-all interviews to glossy magazines after you dump them.'

'You think I should have them sign a confidentiality clause before I take them to bed?'

'I don't know, Luis—I'm your housekeeper, not your counsellor.'

Turning her head, she peered out of the window as the car ascended a terrifyingly narrow road which spiralled its way up a dizzyingly high, green mountain. 'Gosh, it's so beautiful out there,' she said.

'Are you deliberately changing the subject, Carly?'

'I might be.'

He laughed. 'Ever been to Europe before?'

She watched as a bright scarlet sports car squeezed past them in the opposite direction, screwing up her eyes as she wondered if it would make it. 'Just a package holiday to Spain—two weeks in Benidorm in a hotel with my mother and my sister. It was fairly…basic.'

'Then you may be in for something of a treat,' he commented drily as his phone began to ring and, pulling it from his pocket, he answered in Spanish.

The rest of the journey passed quickly and Carly wondered what her sister would say if she could see her now, in a chauffeur driven car, travelling through some of the most expensive real estate in the world. She probably wouldn't have believed it. Come to think of it, she was having a bit of difficulty believing it herself.

The car rounded a bend and she caught her first glimpse of Luis's house—a *belle-époque* villa which he told her he'd bought from an Arabian prince, a friend of a friend, who just happened to be a sultan.

For Carly, it was yet another illustration of his rarefied life, a life which she'd seen only fragments of before. But suddenly it was being pieced together in front of her eyes, like some kind of rich and lavish jigsaw puzzle. He knew sultans and kings. Supermodels and politicians converged on his houses like flocks of glamorous butterflies. But he had no real base, she realised. He flitted from gorgeous house to gorgeous house, but there was no place to call home. Despite all his expensive real estate, Luis Martinez was nothing but a rich and pampered gypsy.

She looked up at the villa as their car drove through the gates, thinking it was like some kind of sumptuous fortress. Dazzling white and shielded by tall dark cypress trees, it sat high in the hills overlooking little azure coves and inlets.

'Are there many staff?' she asked, suddenly nervous.

'Just the usual. And your French counterpart is called Simone. You'll like her.'

Simone was waiting to greet them in a vast reception area with corridors leading off in different directions, like the spokes of a wheel. Tall vases filled with orange roses and spears of eucalyptus were reflected back in large ornate mirrors. A classical statue of a young woman tipping water over herself stood in one corner.

Carly looked around, thinking that it was a bit like being in a museum and that his French housekeeper was scarily chic. Simone's grey dress skated over her slim figure, her hair was cleverly tinted, and, though she must have been pushing fifty, Carly suddenly felt shabby in comparison.

'I'm going straight to my study,' said Luis. 'To

answer some of Diego's increasingly hysterical emails, before he blows a fuse. Simone, this is Carly's first time in France.' He ran his finger thoughtfully over his broken nose. 'I think we might put her in the blue room overlooking the bay.'

There was a split second of hesitation. 'But might Mademoiselle Conner not disturb you, if your rooms are so close?' Simone's smile was fixed. 'I have made up one of the guest houses in the grounds, which might be more…suitable.'

'Carly hasn't travelled in Europe very much before. We might as well give her a decent view.' His eyes were as flat as hammered black metal. 'That won't be a problem, will it?'

'Mais non!' Simone gave a little wiggle of her hands. *'Pas de problème.'*

Carly realised that Luis was watching her and found her cheeks growing warm beneath that hard-eyed scrutiny. And suddenly she was conscious of something more than *consideration* in his dark eyes. Was he looking *at* her, rather than through her, or was she starting to imagine things? She felt her breasts growing heavy and her cheeks flushing, and she thought she saw his eyes gleam in response. *As if he had guessed what she was thinking.*

'That's very kind of you,' she said awkwardly.

'It's nothing. Enjoy the view. I'll see you later. Massage after lunch?'

'As long as it's not a heavy lunch.'

'You see how *stern* she can be, Simone?' he questioned mockingly. 'Don't worry, Carly, I will allow you to police what I eat, if it makes you feel better.'

His words only increased Carly's confused feelings. Was she misreading the signs again, thinking that he was flirting with her? Thinking that a man like him would be looking at someone like *her* with hunger in his eyes? But no matter how much the logical side of her brain tried to tell her that she was mistaken, her instincts were telling her that she was right. His eyes *had* grown smoky with something like desire and she wondered if Simone had picked up on it, too.

She watched as he walked off down the corridor, thinking how much he had improved. She doubted he would need that stick for much longer…soon he would be back to his fighting fit and glorious best.

She swallowed. And when he was? What then? She supposed she would just go back to ironing his sheets and keeping the house in a constant state of readiness for his infrequent visits. It would be as if this whole bizarre interlude had never happened.

And it would be better that way, she told herself fiercely. She wouldn't have to run her hands over his oiled flesh any more, nor feel droplets of water splashing on her skin as he broke through the surface of the water to emerge beside her in the pool, like some dark sea lion. They could slip back into that other, infinitely less threatening relationship they'd had before. The one where she just faded into the background of his busy life and he barely noticed her. And this would all be like a distant dream….

'I shall give you a quick tour,' said Simone. 'Though I warn you that the house can be a little overwhelming on a first visit. Don't worry about your suitcase—someone will take it to your room.'

She followed the Frenchwoman along one of the long corridors, trying to remember what led where, but as Simone had said—the place was a little overwhelming. Doors led off into high rooms most of which overlooked the sea. Carly counted two dining rooms, one with a glass ceiling, which Simone told her could be retracted to open up to the sky. On the ground floor was a gym leading out onto a large pool area with terrace, and on the upper floor was another terrace offering a wrap-around view over the mountains which towered over the back of the house. She thought it was the most beautiful place she'd ever seen.

When at last she was shown to her room, Carly stood open-mouthed trying to take in the Mediterranean view, and a bed made up with linen so white that she felt she'd have to scrub her skin before she dared climb in between the sheets.

'And this,' said Simone, 'is where you'll be staying.'

Suddenly, she could understand the Frenchwoman's reservations about putting her here, because it was a room which was fit for a king. And Luis had given it to *her*. Carly could feel a stupid lump rising in her throat. 'Here?' she questioned, horrified to hear the crack in her voice. 'You mean, I'm staying in here?'

'Yes, here,' said Simone, her voice now sounding almost gentle. 'I will leave you to change. Lunch will be served on the smaller terrace, just after two. Can you remember how to find your way back there?'

'I...think so.'

But after the housekeeper had gone, Carly walked around like someone in a trance, running her fingertips over the billowing white drapes which framed the fabulous view. Out on the terrace, there was a table and chairs and even a lounger. She would be able to read her textbooks out here *and* get some sun.

In the bathroom toiletries were lined up, like in some upmarket department store. Lavender-infused bath salts stood next to a big old-fashioned tub. Thick, soft towels lay in neat piles, like drifts of clouds. There was even a little vase of white freesia perfuming the air. Carly buried her nose in the petals. Flowers in the bathroom—imagine that! Another wave of emotion hit her and, try as she might, she couldn't seem to put the brakes on it.

Because for the first time in her life she didn't feel like second best. Like the geeky child who always dressed in practical clothes while her sister floated around in pretty little dresses. That same geeky child was now staying in a billionaire's home, in a fancy suite of rooms which had clearly been designed to accommodate his upmarket friends. She wondered what Bella and her mother would say if they could see her now.

But as she began to unpack the contents of her

suitcase, she realised that this temporary change of circumstances didn't really change anything. You couldn't make a silk purse out of a sow's ear. She remembered what her mother used to say: *Oh, Carly's got the brains, but Bella's got the beauty.* And to her mother, appearances had been everything.

Carly looked around. Everything here was top of the range—all sleek and clean and shining. Everything except her. The full-length mirror reflected back a woman with a hot face, crumpled clothes and untidy hair. Was she really insane enough to imagine that Luis had been looking at her with *desire*?

She glanced at her watch. Surely she could do *something* with her appearance. If she got a move on then at least she could wash her hair and change into something more presentable for lunch.

But she still felt like an alien as she stripped off and stood beneath the cool shower, self-consciously aware of her fleshy body as she applied creamy soap and shampoo. Afterwards, she blasted her hair dry and had just pulled on a clean set of bra and pants, when there was a knock on the door.

Perhaps it was Simone. Grabbing her discarded towel and holding it in front of her, she walked over to the door and pulled it open.

But it wasn't Simone who stood there.

Carly felt as if someone had just pulled the rug from beneath her feet because suddenly her knees felt shaky.

It was Luis.

Luis, whose black hair was ruffled and damp—presumably because he was fresh out of the shower, just like her. Luis, whose fine linen shirt was clinging to his torso, outlining every hard sinew. And suddenly her perception of him underwent a dramatic shift. This was the man whose half-naked body had become almost normal to her. So why did the fully dressed version suddenly seem way too intimate? She wondered what it was about those faded jeans and damp hair which made her bones feel as if they had turned to jelly. As if she were in danger of melting at his feet.

Because wasn't that what all women did around him? What she had sworn she would *never* do?

Her fingers dug into the soft towel held chastely against her breastbone. She should have felt embarrassed by her own near-naked state. She should tell him she wouldn't be long and close the door on him.

Or *he* should have felt embarrassed at seeing her that way. Shouldn't he apologise for disturbing her and tell her that he'd see her outside on the terrace?

But he didn't.

And neither did she.

They just stood there staring at each other like two people who had just been introduced and she could hear her heart pounding like a drum. Her breasts felt heavy and there was a soft, molten ache between her legs and in the middle of this confusing state came anger, and fear. Because she didn't *do* this kind of stuff. She didn't feel desire any more. She didn't want to. Because desire was unpredictable—and, more importantly, it was *dangerous*.

She shook her head slightly. 'I didn't hear the bell,' she said, licking her dry lips.

He frowned. 'What bell?'

Act normal, she told herself. Pretend that nothing's happening. Because nothing is. 'The lunch bell.'

His eyes narrowed. 'That's because nobody's rung it.'

'Oh. Right. Did you…' she shrugged her shoulders, telling herself this was crazy, but still she stayed rooted to the spot '…er…did you get all your emails answered?'

'No.'

'Diego won't be very pleased.'

'I imagine he won't,' he agreed drily. 'But right now I'm not really thinking about Diego.'

'Oh. R-right.'

Luis felt his throat grow as dry as sandpaper and even her stumbled response didn't dissolve his growing hunger. He knew he should leave *right now* but he couldn't seem to drag his eyes away from her. Not because she looked particularly sexy, because she didn't. Her pale legs and faded bra straps were unremarkable and, for him, it was no big deal to think that beneath that towel she was almost naked. He was used to naked women.

But this was Carly and, for once, her long hair was loose. Freed of the usual tight ponytail, it looked like silk and smelt of bay leaves and he found himself wanting to run his fingers through it. To twist one thick strand possessively around his wrist and to draw her head close enough to kiss her. He wondered what those unpainted lips would taste like. He wondered how the lush curves of her generous body would feel if they were moulded against him.

But it was more than that which drew him. More than the rampant and unexpected lust which was raging around inside him, and a sexual frustration which was making him ache.

She looked clean. That was it. Clean and pure. Her face was untouched by artifice and her iced-tea eyes were wide and dark. She looked like snow before it got trampled on. Before it became all grey and slushy.

And he was the kind of man who did the trampling, wasn't he? He stamped on women's hearts and hardly even noticed he was doing it. He was cruel and insensitive—that was what they said. And she was the last kind of woman he should be lusting after.

But none of that seemed to matter. All he could think about was the aching in his groin which felt as if he were about to *explode*. 'Carly,' he said unsteadily, even though he hadn't been planning to say her name like that.

Her eyes widened. She licked her lips again and made them gleam. 'What's…wrong?'

Her words whispered over his skin like silk and suddenly Luis found himself fighting temptation as he'd never had to fight it before. In the past, if he wanted a woman—he would simply take her, if she was willing. And they were always willing.

But even though her lips had parted with unconscious longing, she was staff, and everyone knew that sleeping with your staff was a recipe for disaster. Even if she weren't, she was all *wrong* for a man like him. She was caring and wholesome. She was the clean light to the darkness which filled the space where once he'd had a soul. What right did he have to mess with her? To take her just because he could and then to leave her broken-hearted afterwards?

'No, nothing's wrong,' he said abruptly. 'I thought I'd show you the way to lunch because I know how easy it is to get lost in this place, but, as usual, you're late. What is it with you?' He scowled at her. 'I'll meet you on the upper terrace in fifteen minutes—and for God's sake, get a move on.'

CHAPTER FIVE

THE INCIDENT AT her bedroom door unsettled her more than it should have done. Carly told herself that Luis had seen her in the swimming pool loads of times so a glimpse of her unexciting bra strap was hardly likely to send him into paroxysms of delight.

But while she might not be very experienced, neither was she stupid. She could read people and their body language—they were two of the traits which made her believe that one day she might make a good doctor. And she had *seen* the way he had looked at her when she'd stood wrapped in her towel. That hadn't been shock or revulsion she'd seen in the Argentinian playboy's eyes, it had been hunger—potent and powerful and almost tangible.

And hadn't she felt it, too? Hadn't what had

silently passed between them made her feel as if she were being swept away by something? As if some dark and invisible wave were dragging her towards something outside her control? She found herself thinking how cruel nature could be, that her body should be so attracted to someone who was out of bounds for about a million different reasons.

She knew her cheeks were still flushed as she joined Luis for lunch that day and she knew, too, that something between them had changed. That no matter how hard she focused her mind, she couldn't seem to make things the same as they'd been before.

Suddenly a new and achingly raw awareness had sprung up between them. She tried not to let it affect her work, but how could it not? The nervous trembling of her fingers when she massaged him reminded her of the first time she'd done it. She found herself missing the confidence which she'd acquired with practice. But what she mourned most was the loss of the ease between them. When for a while she'd felt as if they were almost equals. When she could say exactly what was on her mind and sometimes even make him laugh.

Now there was a terrible and fraught kind of *atmosphere* whenever they were alone. Their curious alliance must have been more fragile than she'd thought or maybe she really *was* naïve after all. Because now he seemed to go out of his way to avoid her unless absolutely necessary, closeting himself in his study and immersing himself in work and leaving Carly largely to her own devices.

Their days settled into an awkward kind of routine. Carly woke early and swam in the pool, long before any of the other staff were around, slightly worried that it might appear presumptuous of her to be enjoying the 'facilities'. She would swim furiously in an attempt to rid herself of the night-time demons which had been haunting her. And afterwards, she would lie floating on her back, looking up as the sun rose higher in the blue sky.

After that, she would take Luis through his

exercises and give him a fairly rigorous massage before breakfast—a pattern she repeated three times throughout the day. And whenever she got the opportunity, she would scuttle away to some largely hidden corner of the vast complex to tackle some reading.

There had been a couple of visitors, each arriving unannounced on separate occasions— Carly had heard their giggles long before she'd seen them. A beautiful blonde and a foxy-looking redhead, who had sat wearing big sun hats and tiny bikinis, draping themselves around the pool without ever managing to get themselves wet.

And Carly had forced herself to stem the unreasonable jealousy which had risen up inside her. She told herself that, *of course*, Luis would have women round—he usually did—and she should be glad that he was showing very obvious signs of complete recovery. Though she noticed that neither woman stayed the night. Each was dispatched home in one of his luxury cars, usually a sign that he was bored.

He had been out a couple of times, too. His driver had taken him along the coast to Monaco, where, according to Simone, a Hollywood actress had taken over a famous restaurant to give a lunch in his honour.

That had been the day when Carly had uninterestedly pushed her *salade Niçoise* around her plate, telling herself not to behave like a possessive child. Of course he would leave her behind! Or had she really pictured herself bursting in on some glamour lunch wearing one of her pastel-coloured T-shirts with her knee-length denim skirt?

At least she'd managed to get through two books she'd been meaning to read for ages, and the fresh air, good food and regular exercise meant that, physically, she felt better than she'd done in a long time, despite her lack of sleep.

One afternoon, her thoughts were travelling along the fascinating labyrinth of quantum physics when a dark shadow fell over the page and she glanced up to see Luis blocking out the light. Behind him the turquoise waters of the infinity pool danced in the sunlight and beyond that was the infinitely darker blue of the sea. But the only things she noticed were his powerful body and that battered straw hat he always wore in the sunshine, and her mouth dried.

'What are you reading?'

She screwed up her eyes, wishing her heart would stop doing that noisy, drum-like thing. Wishing that by now she would have acquired some sort of immunity to him. 'I didn't know it was time for your massage,' she replied.

'That's an odd title for a book.'

'Very funny.' She held up the cover so he could see it.

'And why are you lying in the sunshine reading...' he narrowed his eyes, and read '..."*Quantum Theory Cannot Hurt You*"?'

'Stop laughing at me. You know why. I told you before that I like science.'

'I like cars, but I don't spend my time lolling round the pool reading maintenance manuals. There are plenty of novels in the library—just help yourself.'

'Thanks, but I don't particularly want to read a novel. This is…'

'What?' He lifted his walking stick and used it to point at the dog-eared dust jacket. 'Heavy? Indecipherable?'

'Completely fascinating,' she said quietly. 'In my opinion.'

He rested his stick against one of the sunbeds and gave short laugh. 'You know, you really are something of an enigma, Carly. What are you planning to do with all these qualifications you keep accumulating? Sooner or later, you're surely going to run out of exams to take.'

She hesitated. 'And is there something the matter with that?'

He gave a shrug. 'You'll just become one of those people with a stack of diplomas you never use.'

'Who says I'll never use them?'

He smiled. 'Science may make you *understand* why cornstarch is vital when making *alfajores,* but it isn't really necessary, is it?'

Carly felt a stir of resentment as she met the

mocking question in his eyes, because wasn't that just *typical* of him? There was no praise or even a glimmer of surprise that his house-keeper should have been working hard at exams as she went about her lowly job. It hadn't even occurred to him that she might want more from life than this. The world revolved around Luis, didn't it? Stung by his attitude, she turned on him.

'Maybe I'm not just stockpiling certificates,' she retorted. 'Maybe I'm going to use the exams to make something of myself.'

'Like what?'

'Like, a doctor.'

'You? A doctor?'

Any momentary doubt that it might not be a good idea to tell your employer you were plan-ning on leaving immediately dissolved. Was he arrogant enough to think that she'd be fulfilled for the rest of her life keeping house for him and making sure his favourite cakes were on the table whenever he was in town? Watching and waiting in the background while he lived his life, without having any real life of her own.

'Why not?' she flared. 'Do you think I'm incapable of being a medic?'

'I hadn't really given it a lot of thought.'

What he meant was that he hadn't given *her* a lot of thought. Oh, he might have felt the odd flickering of desire—because she was a woman of child-bearing age who was closeted up with him, and that was how nature had programmed him to react. But he didn't really think about her as a *person*.

Carly stared at him. 'If you must know, I've already applied for medical school and I have a deferred place waiting for me. I'm planning on going just as soon as I've saved up enough money to support myself during the course. I've dreamt about being a doctor for a long time and I don't intend to give up on my dreams any time soon.'

She sat up and pushed her sunglasses on top of her head, but the jiggling movement of her breasts seemed to have distracted him. Or maybe he'd just grown bored with hearing about her dreams. Whatever the reason, he was suddenly staring at her as if he couldn't drag his gaze away. He was staring at her and glaring as if he liked what he saw and yet resented feeling that way—all at the same time.

'You've got a tan,' he said.

Following the direction of his gaze, she glanced down to see the glimpse of white where her shoulder strap had shifted. 'A bit.' She smiled, trying for a little levity to lighten the heavy atmosphere which had suddenly descended on them. 'That is what tends to happen when you expose your skin to the sun, Luis.'

'And you've lost weight.'

'Have I?'

Their eyes met. 'You know you have.'

'If I have, it wasn't intentional.' She shrugged. 'This climate doesn't…well, it doesn't give me much of an appetite, and Simone's been serving those delicious salads. And I've been swimming every morning—in this weather it seems criminal not to. All that helps.'

There was another factor, of course. One which she wouldn't be confiding in him any time soon—and the main reason why her normally healthy appetite seemed to have deserted her.

She wondered what he would say if he knew. If he'd be shocked to learn that these days she had grown to dread and long for their massage sessions, in equal measure. That just the thought of going anywhere near his warm skin started a terrible aching deep inside her. And it was getting worse. She found her hands wanting to linger on his flesh. She wanted to bend her head to the base of his neck and kiss the dark tendrils which curled there. She wondered how her attitude towards men and sex could have changed so radically. Was it possible that all her hard-wired fears of intimacy had been melted by daily exposure to Luis Martinez and his magnificent body?

'Don't you own a bikini?'

His impatient question startled her and Carly looked at him. 'A bikini?'

'You know, the garment of choice for most women your age rather than something your grandmother might be seen wearing.'

Her cheeks grew hot as she looked down to where her thighs were outlined against the cushions of the sunlounger. 'I'm the wrong sort of shape for a bikini.'

'And what sort of shape is that?'

She lifted her gaze to his. 'Too fat.'

'You are not too fat,' he said impatiently. 'You're curvy, yes—but in all the right places. And men like curves. Actually, they like to see them, instead of them being hidden away behind shapeless clothes which are deeply unflattering.' His mouth hardened. 'You ought to give it a try some time. Stop moaning about the way you look and try doing something to change it, if it makes you unhappy.'

'You do say the nicest things, Luis.'

'Maybe it was something you needed to hear,' he said, unrepentantly.

She snapped her book shut. 'What time is it?'

'Ten after four.'

'Then we'd better go for your massage.'

'If you say so, Carly.'

'I do say so.'

But Luis didn't move. He couldn't. Because massage was the last thing he was thinking about right then. From here all he could see were her legs. Legs which had turned a shade of the *dulce de leche* he used to eat as a child. A paler shade than the syrupy sweet which used to seep out from the *facturas* pastries his mother used to make—back in the days before betrayal had slipped its lethal knife into his world and changed it for ever.

He felt that familiar little stab of pain but it was overridden by the infinitely sharper spiralling of lust. He dragged his gaze away from her legs but today she was like a beacon who seemed to glow golden just about everywhere. Even her hair had caught the sun and there were pale licks of colour nestling in amid the sedate brown, making it look as if she'd spent hours at an expensive hairdresser's. He shifted his position a little, but it had little effect on the heavy aching at his groin.

'Give me fifteen minutes,' he said tersely. 'I need to make a phone call first.'

'Fifteen minutes it is.' She scrambled up from the lounger as if she couldn't wait to get away from him. 'I'll see you in the massage room.'

He watched her go and the sway of her hips made him harder still. Her swimsuit was riding up and revealing more of her bottom than she probably would have liked, if only she'd been aware of it. He suspected she would be appalled if she knew just how much of her creamy buttocks he could see, because she was a prude, no question. She dressed like a prude and she acted like one, too.

Yet he knew enough about women to realise that she was as jumpy as a box of newly lit fireworks whenever he was around. And then some. Did she think he was blind to the way her cheeks went pink whenever he walked unexpectedly into the room? Her newly acquired tan wasn't deep enough to conceal *that*. Did she think he hadn't noticed that her breasts were diamond-nubbed and straining, whenever they were in the pool together? Or that during his massage sessions her hands had gone back to that same trembling she'd had at the beginning.

It was a powerful kind of chemistry, and if it had been anyone other than Carly she would have made a pass at him by now. And in truth, that probably would have been enough to deflate his interest—or certainly to cut it short. The easy lay had never been a problem; it was the potentially unobtainable which had always intrigued him. He realised that he'd never met anyone who had actively fought her attraction to him before. It was incredibly...arousing.

Propping his walking stick against the lounger, he pulled his cell phone from the pocket of his robe and called his office in Argentina. For a while he allowed his mind to be taken over with the practical considerations of his business empire, while his assistant read out the list of bullet points she had prepared for him. Most concerned his global building projects: the luxury apartments being constructed on Uruguay's most beautiful beach and the new hospital in Santiago del Estero. As he listened to her neat summary, he realised that everything was going according to plan. The conservation measures he was instigating in the south of his country had been so successful that he'd been asked to chair a Pan-European convention in the fall.

But as he mentally filed away the information he was given, different images started crowding into his mind. Images which were painful and unwelcome. He tried to block them out, just as he'd spent the last four months blocking them, but for once it wasn't working. He stared at his walking stick and suddenly found himself remembering the accident with a crystal clarity which made him flinch.

It was all too easy to recall that strange split second of calm, moments before impact. And then the deafening crumple of metal as his car had smashed into the side of the track. He closed his eyes as he remembered the stench of burning rubber and the first hot lick of flames as the car had ignited around him. The distant sirens and muffled shouts of his rescuers had grown louder with their sense of urgency and panic. He remembered being trapped in that metal coffin, thinking that he was about to die.

And if he had died? What would he have had to show for his life? A bloated bank account and a shelf full of trophies. His mouth hardened. It wasn't much of a legacy, was it?

The sound of a bird calling out from one of the trees brought him back to the present. He looked around at the luxury pool and the villa which rose like an elaborate white cake out of the tiered green gardens. Dusky-pink roses and starry-white jasmine scented the air and his senses suddenly felt saturated. How beautiful it was, he thought, and, ultimately, how fragile. It could all be over in a heartbeat.

Couldn't it?

He felt something flicker and power into life inside him as he began walking towards the massage room, like a man in a trance.

Quietly opening the door, he blinked against

the subdued light to see Carly with her back to him, lining up bottles of aromatic oils in a neat row. He stared at the set of her shoulders and the ponytail which hung down her back and he knew the exact moment when she heard him enter, for her long fingers stilled on a small vial which looked like some alchemist's potion. She had changed into her uniform and the ice-blue dress stretched across the broad beam of her bottom, emphasising its generous curves.

He also knew the exact moment when his painful recall became transmuted into desire. Only this time it wasn't the low-grade variety which had been nagging away at him for weeks. Suddenly it was gathering all the force of a tidal wave—whipped up by soft *dulce de leche* flesh and eyes the colour of iced tea.

He could smell the subtle bayleaf scent of her hair as she turned round and flicked her ponytail back and the gesture made her breasts jiggle beneath the uniform dress. Automatically, his gaze lingered on them and it took all his concentration to lift his eyes to her face.

'You…startled me,' she said.

'That wasn't my intention.'

'Where's your stick?'

With a start he looked down at his empty hands, only just noticing that he'd left it behind. 'I didn't even realise,' he said. 'I must have left it by the pool.'

'I'll go and get it for you.'

'No,' he said suddenly. 'I don't need it any more.'

'I think that's something your doctor should decide.'

'My doctor's not here, Carly.' He began to walk across the room towards her. And suddenly he was walking completely unaided, consciously free of support for the first time in months and he gave a low shout of laughter at the sense of exhilaration he felt. 'But you are.'

'I'm not qualified to give medical advice.'

'I don't need any medical advice,' he said, his shadow falling over her face as he came to a halt right in front of her. 'At least, not for what I'm planning to do.'

'Oh? And what's that?' she questioned lightly, as if there weren't a hundred dark undercurrents flowing between them. As if her darkened eyes weren't unconsciously begging for him to kiss her.

'You're an intelligent woman, Carly. Don't ask questions to which you already know the answer.'

Her eyes were huge as she looked at him, but they were wary, too. She shook her head and he could see the rippling movement of her throat before she spoke, as if she were trying to swallow something which was stuck there. 'I don't know what you're talking about.'

'Oh, please. Don't *pretend*, Carly. You're too clever for that. Unless you're trying to deny the chemistry which has been building for weeks, or that you want to kiss me as much as I want to kiss you. You're driving me out of my mind with frustration, and I have the feeling that if I don't do something about it soon, then one or both of us are going to go crazy.'

Carly was trembling as he reached out and

coiled his fingers around the back of her head and the unthreatening nature of the gesture meant that she found herself sinking into it. And once she had let him touch her, she was lost. She tried to think logically. To be that person who was good at science. To concentrate on the million reasons why this shouldn't happen. But all she could think of was how mesmerising it felt to have the tips of his fingers rubbing at her scalp like that, as if he was giving her an impromptu head massage. As if the tables had turned and he was the one now in charge. Oh, yes. He was definitely the one in charge. She could feel her eyelashes fluttering and the lids suddenly felt unbearably heavy. 'We can't do this,' she said desperately.

'Why not?'

'You know why not. I work for you—'

'I'll give you dispensation, starting from now.'

'That's not funny.'

'It wasn't intended to be funny. I've never been more serious.'

He was still stroking her scalp and Carly knew

she should pull away before it was too late. *So why didn't she?* Because she liked his fingers in her hair and his black eyes looking at her like that? Or because all those feelings she'd thought were dead were now flickering to life inside her, and she was afraid to move in case they disappeared again?

Their eyes met and held.

'We can't,' she said again, more desperately this time.

'Stop fighting it. We can do any damned thing we like,' he said harshly as he pulled her face towards his.

But unlike his words, his kiss was soft. Soft and insistent and innocent enough to make her relax, until she felt her lips parting through no conscious effort of her own. She felt the flicker of his tongue against the roof of her mouth and, automatically, she coiled her arms around him, clinging to him with an eagerness which surprised her. She had watched him and wanted him for weeks and at last she was touching him.

And suddenly she was consumed by her need

for him. The past became nothing but a desolate place which was retreating by the second. The present was here. Now. And she wanted to live every single second of it.

Did she make some kind of sound? Was that why he lifted his head to stare down at her with a gleam of pleasure in his black eyes? His mouth gave a flicker of a smile before he lowered his head towards hers again.

She didn't know how long that second kiss lasted, only that it was underpinned with a new sense of purpose. He levered her up against the wall, pushing the flat of his hand above her head for support, while with the other he stroked her face. And not just her face. His fingers moved down over her neck, drawing tiny little lines along her collarbone, and she shivered in response. Next thing she knew, they were skating down over her breastbone and she moved her body restlessly. She heard him give a soft laugh as he pulled at the zip of her uniform dress. She felt that first little tug of resistance before he slid it down to her waist and the material parted easily, leaving her breasts to slide free.

She felt the rush of air which cooled her skin and heard his muffled murmur of appreciation as he drew away to look at her. He didn't seem to notice her functional bra—nor to care that it was chosen with support rather than frivolity in mind. There was nothing but dark intensity on his face and a look in his eyes she'd never seen there before.

'*Perfecta,*' he uttered, cupping one breast in the palm of his hand, as if he was weighing it. His thumb flickered across one nipple and, despite the barrier of the bra, her puckered flesh tightened in a rush of pure pleasure.

'Oh!' she gasped.

'Still think we "can't"?' he mocked.

She couldn't think of anything except the way he was making her feel. His hand had slithered down to her dress and he was rucking it up. Her body felt hot. Her skin was suddenly too tight for her body and her pounding heart too big for her chest. She closed her eyes, hardly daring to breathe for fear that he would come to his senses, and stop.

But he showed no signs of stopping. On the contrary, he was now pushing her towards the narrow massage bed, which lay like a sacrificial table at the centre of the room, and she felt her bottom collide with the soft, leather surface. Instinctively, she dug her fingers into his neck, terrified that she was going to slip to the floor and take him with her and shatter all the sensual magic. Momentarily, his mouth curved into a hard smile.

'Relax,' he murmured. 'I wouldn't be doing this if I didn't think I was capable of following through.'

The sexual boast broke into the sweet fug of desire which had descended on her and the magic began to dissolve in a way which was chillingly familiar. Her body went from heated need to icy revulsion in one sobering second. Only this time she wasn't with some sleaze of a guy at a party, who was still smarting with rage at another woman's rejection. This was Luis.

Luis her boss.

Luis who bedded actresses and supermodels. *What was she doing?*

Panic swept into her mind like the dark beat of flapping wings. With all the detachment which her scientific brain was capable of, she pictured the scene as others might see it. As Simone might see if she walked into the massage room. Carly with her uniform open to the waist—her breasts hanging out and her legs parted. And her billionaire boss with his hand up her skirt, eager to slake his frustration on the most accommodating woman to hand. Despite her lacklustre looks and lowly job, he had decided that he wanted to have sex with someone as unlikely as *her*. Someone who just happened to be in the right place at the right time.

Or the wrong time.

Appalled at herself, she pushed at his chest with the flat of her hand. 'No!' she said.

Perhaps he thought she was playing a game. As if she had suddenly decided to adopt the role of tease, because he dipped his head to brush his lips over hers. 'Oh, Carly,' he said, very softly. 'Just shut up and kiss me again.'

But the kiss was no longer working. It no longer felt like magic. Her mind was playing tricks with her as she started to remember that other kiss. The forced entry of an alien tongue, and then...then... The blood in her veins was now so icy that it hurt.

'No,' she said again, splaying the flat of her hand over his chest.

And maybe this time he realised she meant it. That her words weren't just the flutter of someone saying something because they felt they should. She could see surprise flickering over his face, as if nobody had ever stopped him before, and she wondered how she could have been so stupid.

Of course nobody had ever stopped him before.

She slid down from the massage bed but her fingers were shaking as she yanked the zip of her dress back up and tugged her skirt into place.

'What are you doing?' he demanded.

'What does it l-look like? I'm calling a halt to this before it gets completely out of hand.'

'I don't understand. One minute you're up for it, and the next you're acting like I'm the big, bad wolf.' His face darkened. 'I'm not crazy about women who play games. What's the matter, Carly?'

'What's the *matter*?' Moving away, she gripped onto the aromatherapy table for support, her heart racing so hard that she felt dizzy. 'Where shall I begin? With the total lack of professionalism we've both just demonstrated?'

'I told you that I was prepared to overlook that.'

Carly shook her head. She never got it right where men were concerned, did she? Maybe she was just one of those women who had *victim* or *walkover* written all over them. She looked at Luis, at his magnificent body in the faded jeans and white shirt and the way his sensual mouth seemed to form a natural, wilful pout. The wild black hair hung in tendrils around his collar and he looked just as much a pin-up as he'd ever been.

As if someone like him would seriously be interested in someone like *her* in normal circumstances. 'Well, I'm not prepared to overlook it,' she said. 'Because no woman likes to think of herself as a substitute.'

His eyes were suddenly watchful. 'What the hell are you talking about?'

'Oh, come on. This is *me*, Luis, not someone you've just picked up at a party. I've been in your life long enough to know what you're like. You're renowned as being a ladies' man. As a man who loves women.'

'Your point being?' he questioned coldly.

'That you're known for your love of supermodels and actresses. In all the time I've worked for you, I've never seen you date someone who…' *Say it, Carly. Just come right out and say it.* 'Someone like me!' she finished. 'Someone ordinary, who you're only making a pass at because I just happen to be around.'

He rubbed his finger up and down the uneven

surface of a nose which had once been broken by a jealous husband, but when he spoke, his voice was curiously calm. 'You don't think I could have one of these leggy *supermodels* or *actresses* in my bed within an hour or two, if I wanted? That it might be more straightforward if I did?'

'So why don't you?' she challenged.

'Because it's you I want,' he said savagely. 'It may be wrong and it may be inexplicable, but I. Want. You. And you want me, too.'

Carly stared at him. His voice had roughened and grown hard with desire, but only one word stood out. His feelings for her were *inexplicable,* were they? He couldn't understand why he wanted her. Yet wasn't he only telling her what she already knew? That this could only ever be a one-off, which was only ever going to end in tears.

And she couldn't let it happen, no matter how much she wanted him.

She wondered how to handle it. She could storm out without any kind of explanation, but that wouldn't solve anything. From what she knew about human psychology, she guessed that flight might only sharpen his decidedly alpha traits. He might be fired up enough to hunt her down and kiss away all her doubts and she might not be strong enough to resist him again.

But if she told him the bare facts, then wouldn't that act as a natural repellent? He was a playboy, yes, but she suspected he had the double standard so common to many of his type. Didn't men like Luis see women as either good girls, or whores? If he knew the truth about her, he might *respect* an innocence which would put her off-limits to him, and stop this from happening ever again.

She met the hungry glitter of his gaze.

'Well, it's not going to happen, because I'm...'

'You're what?'

She tried to swallow down the complex mix of feelings, but suddenly it was no good and the words came spilling out of her mouth. 'I'm a virgin!' she burst out, and saw the narrow-eyed look of comprehension on his face. 'Yes! Now do you understand, Luis? I'm a freak—a weirdo—a twenty-three-year-old woman who has never had sex!'

And with that, she turned and ran from the massage room as if some deadly snake had slithered down from the mountain and was intent on biting her.

CHAPTER SIX

HE DIDN'T COME after her.

He didn't follow her to her sumptuous room overlooking the bright blue bay. He didn't push his way in and try to kiss away every one of her objections, which seemed to be diminishing as the minutes ticked by. Carly stood staring out at the sleek white yachts she could see skimming across the distant water and felt the plummet of her heart. Had she really thought he might? Hadn't she *hoped* he might?

Well, yes. If honesty was the name of the game, she *had*.

She bit her lip as doubt washed over her. Even if Luis had decided that making love to her was a bad idea after what she'd just told him, at least he could have reassured her that she wasn't some sort of freak, even if she'd used that description herself. He could have laughed it all off as behaviour which had just got out of hand. He could tell her what she already knew, that there was definitely chemistry, but that it would be a very bad idea to act on it. Then they could forget what had happened and go back to how it had been before.

She turned away from the window. Could she do that? Pretend that he hadn't kissed her breasts, or rucked up her skirt like that? Or that she hadn't enjoyed every glorious and forbidden second of it, until his boast reminded her just what kind of man she was dealing with.

Walking over to the mirror, she saw herself as Luis must have seen her. Her skin was flushed, her hair wild and her eyes didn't look like her eyes any more. She swallowed. This was a Carly she didn't recognise.

A Carly she'd thought was lost for ever. A woman who could feel desire and act on it, just like any other woman.

Throwing her discarded uniform into the laundry basket, she washed her face and changed, but as she brushed her hair and tied it back into a ponytail she wondered how she was going to fill the hours until supper. And what on earth she was going to say to Luis when she saw him again. How *could* she have told him about her virginity like that?

Her muddled thoughts were disturbed by a knock on the door and her dread was complicated by the thunder of her heart when she opened it to find Luis standing there.

But on his face wasn't the anger she had been anticipating. Wasn't that a trace of *amusement* she could read in his dark eyes?

'You have to realise,' he said drily, 'that if you want a man to run after you, it's usually better to choose a man who can actually run.'

She swallowed. 'I didn't want you to run after me.'

'Oh, but I think you did,' he said, dark eyebrows rising. 'Aren't you going to invite me in?'

'I don't think that's a good idea.'

'You have a better one? Like pretending nothing happened?'

'Nothing *did* happen.'

'No?'

She shook her head. 'No!'

His eyes narrowed. 'Look, why don't you open the door properly and let me in, so that we can have this conversation in private?'

'Is that an order?'

'If that's what it takes—then yes, it's an order.'

Carly hesitated, but she could see from his expression that he wasn't going anywhere. He wanted to satisfy his curiosity. He wanted to know *why* and at the end of the day he was still her boss, wasn't he? If they *had* to have this conversation then surely it was better without the risk of Simone or one of the other staff coming past and overhearing them.

'Oh, very well. Come in, if you must,' she said ungraciously, opening the door wider.

Luis walked into the room, his heart beating out a primitive tattoo as she closed the door behind him. He had just spent the last hour telling himself that this was a bad idea and that he should forget what had almost happened.

But he couldn't forget it. Or maybe he didn't want to. He couldn't forget the look of shame on her face as she'd blurted out her innocence to him. And he couldn't forget the way she'd made him feel when he'd kissed her. It had felt sweet and soft and powerful. But most of all it had felt dangerous, and he had always been hooked on danger.

He heard her footsteps behind him and turned to look at her. Beneath the light tan her face was tight with tension and she was chewing the inside of her lip. He found himself wanting to take that look of anxiety away. He wanted to make her melt again, only this time, he wanted to do it slowly.

'So why are you here, Luis?'

'Not to apologise, if that's what you're thinking.'

She seemed to have difficulty meeting his gaze. 'Then, why?' she whispered.

'I want to know why you spoke about your virginity like that.'

She flinched, as if his bluntness had startled

her, but she treated his question in the same way she might have treated a polite enquiry about the weather. 'And how was that?'

'As if you were ashamed of it.'

Now some of her poise seemed to desert her because she stared at the floor and started rubbing her toe against the Persian carpet. There was a long pause before she lifted her head to meet his gaze. 'Why should that surprise you?' she said. 'It's not exactly something to be proud of, is it? We live in an age where we're bombarded by sexual images, and people who don't conform to the norm of having amazing sex all the time are regarded as freaks. Most women of twenty-three aren't like me.'

'You make it sound like a burden,' he said.

'In many ways, it is.'

He narrowed his eyes. 'Yet when I gave you the opportunity to liberate yourself from this state of self-imposed purdah, you turned and ran away.'

Her knuckles clenched. 'It was very generous of you to offer to "liberate" me,' she hissed.

'But I'm not some *charity case,* eager for the big stud Martinez to show me where I've been going wrong all this time.'

He raised his eyebrows. 'And where have you been *going wrong?*'

'It doesn't matter.'

'Yes, it does.'

'Please don't push it, Luis.'

'Why not? I think you should talk about it.'

And suddenly all the fight seemed to leave her. Her shoulders slumped as she sat down heavily on the edge of the bed and looked up at him. 'What do you want to know?'

'Everything.'

'That's a big ask.'

'I know it is.'

For almost a minute Carly didn't speak, trying to convince herself that he had no right to demand to know these things. Until she reminded herself that she had started the ball rolling. She had told him or, at least, told him some of it. She must have realised that someone like Luis would demand to know the full story.

She hadn't talked about it for years. Not since it had happened. She had taken it and buried it in a dark place somewhere deep inside her. She hardly ever thought about it now, only when she awoke from those occasional nightmares, the ones where she was clutching her throat and unable to breathe. Did that mean that on some subconscious level it still troubled her? And mightn't it be good to get it off her chest to someone, even if that someone just happened to be her boss?

'So why, Carly?'

His soft question slid in through all her defences, and suddenly she was back there. Back with those lights flashing and music pounding and that horrible dizzy feeling, which had ended with her bent double at the bottom of a frosty garden, being sick into one of the flower beds. In the bright, sunlit bedroom of the luxury Mediterranean villa, it seemed as if it had all happened to someone else. But it had happened to her.

'I was at a party,' she said tonelessly.

'When?'

'I was sixteen, but I probably looked older. I hadn't been out of the house for weeks because of Dad, so I went with a schoolfriend to this big party on the edge of town. For once, I was wearing make-up and I'd borrowed some of my friend's clothes and I felt excited. And there was this…this guy…' She stumbled over her words, trying to present them in the fairest possible light. Because hadn't she asked herself again and again if she'd somehow *deserved* what had happened to her? Wasn't that what women always did in situations like this? 'I'd had a couple of drinks—and so had he. He'd probably had a bit more than a couple, come to think of it.'

'So he was drunk?'

'A bit,' she said. 'But mostly he was just in love with someone else. Someone who didn't want him.'

'You're not making any sense, Carly.'

'Aren't I?' she said and she gave a hollow kind of laugh. 'Okay, then, I'll spell it out for you. I was supposed to be his substitute lover for that evening, though I didn't know it at the time. I was the lucky person he'd picked to make him feel better about himself. To make him know that he was still desired. Surely you can guess what happened next?'

'Oh, I can guess, but I'd rather be told.' His mouth had grown hard. 'You say you want to be a doctor. Well, you'll make a much better doctor if you don't cling onto the past and use it like some kind of security blanket.'

There was a pause which seemed to go on for an uncomfortably long time.

'He started to kiss me,' she said eventually, her voice a stilted whisper. 'And then to touch me. At first I liked it. I liked the way it made me feel. But then….'

'Then what, Carly?'

His words sounded distant. As if they were coming from somewhere far away.

'He…' She winced with pain and shame. She could almost feel those fingers probing her, digging into her dryness and telling her she should have been wet. Telling her that she was frigid and useless. The clamp of those teeth was sharp on her breasts and the sound of her knickers being ripped apart seemed deafening. She had attempted to scream, but he had blotted out the scream with the vodka-soaked slick of his mouth. 'He…' Her voice shuddered to a halt as, wordlessly, she shook her head.

'*Raped* you?'

His appalled question broke the spell and Carly opened eyes she didn't even realise had been closed. She shook her head again. 'No. Not that.'

'But he touched you…intimately?'

'Yes.'

'Aggressively?'

'Oh, yes.'

'That's a definition of rape in many of the statute books,' he gritted out and there was a dark anger on his face she'd never seen before. 'What stopped him?'

'Someone came into the room to collect their coat and disturbed us.'

'And then you called the police?'

She didn't answer, not straight away, and in a way wasn't this the bit she was most ashamed of? That she had succumbed to pressure and other people's expectations and allowed them to take control of the situation.

'No. I decided against it.'

'You decided against it?'

'That's what I said.'

There was a split second of a pause. 'Do you want to tell me why?'

Carly met his eyes and their dark light washed over her. Dark light was a contradiction in terms, wasn't it? But that was what she was getting from him. And it was disarming. It was like a deep bath at the end of a long day. Like holding out your cold hands in front of a blazing fire.

'What stopped you from reporting it?' he said.

'My mother did,' she said baldly.

'Your *mother*?'

'She said it would be impossible to prove, that it would be his word against mine, and she had a point. He was insanely rich and well-connected, and could have hired the best defence lawyers. I was just an ordinary girl with a sick father and no money. I wouldn't have stood a chance. My name would have been mud. It would have been just one more thing to add to the stack of dark things which were building up at home. And it wasn't as if he actually *raped* me.'

'But what about the person who came in to collect their coat? Couldn't they have been called as your defence if they witnessed the attack?'

She gave a bitter laugh. 'It was a friend of his,' she said, 'who described it as "horseplay".'

For a moment he winced, as if her pain were his pain. *'Cabrón,'* he bit out, his eyes darkening as he walked over to the bed and sat down beside her.

Carly tensed, but the arm he placed around her shoulder felt protective, not seductive. Although she guessed that in some way it *was* seductive. He seemed to represent safety and she'd never really had that before. She wanted to lean against him and drink it in, but she forced herself not to. She had learnt to stand on her own two feet and she didn't need to lean on anyone, but, even if she did, it certainly shouldn't be Luis, because he was the antithesis of safe. Luis was all about danger.

'So that's when you started sublimating your femininity,' he said slowly.

'I don't know what you're talking about.'

'Oh, I think you do.' He nodded, as if something was suddenly making sense to him. 'That must have been when you started scraping your hair back into that damned ponytail, which means nobody ever gets to see it. Probably around the time when you stopped wearing clothes which might flatter you, or the make-up which most women your age wear. You must have thought that if you didn't draw attention to yourself then you wouldn't attract the wrong kind of attention. That by being invisible, people would look through you rather than at you, and it wouldn't ever happen to you again.'

His perception was unsettling and Carly could

feel the sting of tears at the backs of her eyes. But she blinked them away, because to break down and cry in front of him would be the final humiliation. 'You think that suddenly you're qualified to act as some kind of amateur shrink, just because I've told you my sob story?'

'It's not a sob story, Carly. It's the truth. And I want to help you.'

'Well, I don't want your help,' she said, pulling away from his grasp and staring out at the terrace, where a fat bee was disappearing into the scarlet trumpet of an hibiscus flower.

'You might not want my help.' His voice was quiet. 'But you want me.'

Forcing her attention away from the pollen-brushed bee, she jerked her head round to look at him. Suddenly she realised that she was sitting on a bed next to him and she shouldn't be. She shouldn't be within six feet of him. And she definitely shouldn't be staring into his eyes like that and losing herself in their dark luminosity. 'No, I don't,' she whispered.

'Then try saying it as if you mean it.' His

mouth flickered into a hard smile. 'Except we both know you can't.'

'I can't believe you're saying this. Do you really think it's...*acceptable*...' her voice shook '...to start talking about desire, in the light of what I've just told you?'

'Yes,' he said fiercely. 'Absolutely I do. What happened to you was bad, and the guy who took advantage of you was a piece of scum, but it happened a long time ago and you can't let it write the script for the rest of your life. Sex isn't *wrong,* Carly. It's natural. It's one of the greatest pleasures in life and you're missing out on it. Don't you see that?'

His fierce words were impossible to brush aside and suddenly Carly realised that she felt better for having told him. She felt lighter—*cleaner.* As if she'd scrubbed years of grime away from her skin and stepped out into the sunlight.

And Luis had been the catalyst for that.

She stared at him. 'I'm wondering where we

go from here,' she said. 'Do you think we can we go back to how it's been before?'

'Possibly.' He took one of her hands in his and turned it over, studying her palm as if he was examining her lifeline, and when he looked up again there was a question in his eyes. 'But I don't want to. And neither do you. Not really.'

He had lifted his fingertips to her face and was tracing a feather-light path down over her cheek and Carly had to resist the urge to close her eyes, because it felt so *right* to have him touching her. She swallowed as his thumb moved across the cushion of her bottom lip and suddenly it began to tremble.

'Luis,' she said, but it came out in a way she didn't recognise. As if she was making a protest without really meaning it.

And he smiled, as if he had just won a battle she hadn't even realised they were having, before lowering his voice. 'Tell me something, Carly. Are you saving your virginity for the man you will one day marry?'

His blunt question shook her out of her dreamy

state and she blinked at him in surprise. 'That's a strange question to ask at a time like this.'

He shook his head. 'It's exactly the right question to ask because I need to know what's important to you.'

She wanted to tell him that she wasn't sure she could answer coherently when his thumb was rubbing her lip like that, but she didn't want him to stop. 'Then no. The answer is no. I wasn't *saving* it for anyone. It's not like money you put in the bank. It's just that I'd never met anyone who—'

'Makes you feel the way I do?'

His murmured assertion should have sounded unbearably arrogant, but it didn't. Because that was the truth, too. She shook her head. 'No.'

He leaned forward and replaced his thumb with his lips, brushing them over hers in a way which made her tremble even more.

'I want to be your lover, Carly,' he breathed. 'I want to show you how to enjoy pleasure, for pleasure's sake. You have helped heal me—so let me now heal you.'

'S-sexual healing?' she questioned unsteadily.

'If you like.'

She drew her head away from his. 'It's...it's a crazy idea.'

'Why?'

Why?

A million reasons flooded into her head. Sex wasn't supposed to be something you just *did*, was it, like some cold-blooded experiment carried out in laboratory conditions? Sex was supposed to be about passion. A lot of people thought it was only about *love*.

She looked into the hard gleam of his eyes and suddenly she understood what that journalist had meant when she'd written that article. His face was rugged and beautiful, yes, but his eyes really did look *empty*. As if you could jump into their black depths and never reach the bottom. And surely only a fool would choose to be intimate with a known heartbreaker like Luis Martinez.

Yet the detached, scientific side of her personality was impressed by his honesty. He wasn't spinning her lies by making promises he couldn't fulfil. He was offering to teach her the art of sex.

She imagined turning him down. Of going back to being the woman she'd been before. Carly the invisible. Carly the scared. But she hadn't felt invisible when he'd kissed her. Or scared. She had felt three-dimensional and desired—properly desired—for the first time in her life. Hadn't it come as a huge relief to discover that the creep at the party hadn't destroyed those kind of feelings for ever? That deep down she was still a functioning woman, with a woman's needs.

And didn't she want that? Wasn't it time for her to truly leave the past behind?

'So how would it work?' she questioned casually, but maybe her nonchalant tone didn't fool him because she saw him smile in response. '*If* I were to agree.'

'I hadn't actually given much thought to that,' he said. 'I thought that might have been a little…*presumptuous.*'

'I suppose it might.' But Carly didn't care about *presumptuous*; she just wanted him to begin. She wanted him to kiss her again and make her feel the way she'd done before. She wanted his hands on her breasts and in her hair. She wanted to know what would happen if that low ache deep inside her was allowed to keep building and building...

Letting her eyelashes flicker to a close, she elevated her chin, silently inviting him to kiss her. But his soft laugh made her eyes snap open.

'Oh, no,' he said softly. 'This is not how I intend for your seduction to happen, *querida*. It will not be here, or now. It will not be fast and furious with us grappling on your bed like a couple of greedy teenagers. It will be a slow and considered feast. A banquet guaranteed to satisfy all the senses, rather than something devoured without tasting properly. I want you to be sure that this is what you really want.' His lips curved into a slow smile. 'And when you do, there will be no holds barred.'

She wanted to contradict him. To listen to the

small part of her brain which was questioning her own sanity. But the heat in her blood had other ideas and so she shrugged, as if it were no big deal. 'So...'

'So.' He stood up very quickly, as if he didn't quite trust himself to sit chastely beside her on the bed any more. 'You will meet me on the upper terrace at eight o'clock. I will instruct the chef to prepare something cold and dismiss the staff for the rest of the night. We will not be disturbed.'

A shiver of anticipation whispered over her skin.

'I should like you to wear a skirt or a dress and to leave your legs bare,' he continued. 'Oh, and make sure your hair is down. I don't want to see you with that damned ponytail.'

'Anything else?' she questioned, her sarcasm hiding the sudden hurt she felt.

'Yes. And this is probably the most important provision of all.' He looked down at her, his shadow suddenly enveloping her like a dark cloak. 'I need you to promise that you won't fall in love with me. I can do sex—very good sex, as it happens—but I don't do love. Do you understand, Carly? Because I mean it. And if you think this is going to end in wedding bells and clouds of confetti, then you're mistaken.'

Carly was in no doubt that he meant it. She could tell from the implacable note in his voice and the steely glint of his eyes. And while his arrogance was shocking, once again she couldn't help admiring his honesty. Luis would never spin her any impossible dreams, would he?

'There's no need to worry about that,' she said. 'Believe me, I have no desire to waft up the aisle in a cloud of tulle and then listen to a load of boring speeches. I'm going to be a doctor, not a housewife, and I'm certainly not in any danger of falling in love with you, Luis. I know you too well.'

He smiled. 'That's what I like about you, Carly. I like your clear-headed way of thinking.'

But as Carly looked into the hard glitter of his eyes she suddenly found herself wondering if she had taken on more than she could handle.

CHAPTER SEVEN

CARLY BECAME PROGRESSIVELY more nervous as she got ready for dinner that night. Her mouth had grown dry and her hands were trembling and she thought seriously about abandoning the whole idea and telling Luis it had all been a horrible misunderstanding. Could she really go through with losing her virginity to a man like him, who had laid out his exacting guidelines from the start? She thought about what he'd said about her appearance, about what she should and shouldn't wear for her seduction. He had been positively *brutal* in his assessment of her physical appearance, hadn't he?

Yet he'd said nothing which wasn't true. Dull anonymity had been her aim and it seemed she had achieved exactly that. But while fading into the background had worked brilliantly when she'd been his housekeeper, he had told her quite emphatically that it was inappropriate for her new role...

As what?

His lover?

She licked her lips as she pulled the scrunchy from her hair.

Or just someone who was jumping in way out of her depth?

She soaked in a long bath, then hunted around for something suitable to wear but that made her feel even worse. She had convinced herself that she didn't *care* about pretty clothes, but as she surveyed her plain skirts and T-shirts she wished that someone would suddenly appear with a magic wand and transform her wardrobe into something frivolous and...*pretty.*

She did the best she could, but it wasn't easy for someone who had become a stranger to titillation. She had no idea how to primp herself to look good and gain a man's attention. She hadn't worn make-up in years, and her only jewellery was a tiny pearl on a gold chain, which her granny had given her. She fastened it around her neck with still-shaky fingers, but when she surveyed her completed image in the mirror she knew she couldn't go through with it.

Her mother had been right all along. You really couldn't make a silk purse out of a sow's ear. What would Luis say when he saw her with her scrubbed face and her cheap clothes and a pair of sandals which were currently showcasing her unmanicured toes? How could she possibly trot down to the terrace like some sort of prize pony and prepare to give him her virginity?

She began to pace the room, but that only increased her paranoia. What if she phoned him and told him she'd changed her mind? He might be irritated, yes, but he would understand. *Wouldn't he?* He might even be relieved.

But still she hesitated as she walked over to the bed, where her cell phone sat on the table beside it.

What would she say?

A soft knock on the door was followed by

someone opening it and suddenly Luis was walking into the room. His face was dark with question as his narrow-eyed gaze swept over her.

'Have you started walking in without being invited?' she said.

'I thought I'd better come and find you,' he answered. 'But judging from the expression on your face, your no-show on the terrace might indicate something more than your usual poor timekeeping.'

She shook her head and suddenly she didn't bother to hide her feelings behind a wall of pretending not to care. 'Luis, I *can't.*'

He was walking towards her and she could feel the loud bashing of her heart against her ribcage. Though he was dressed down in jeans and a linen shirt, nothing could disguise the glossy patina of power which moulded itself to him like a second skin. Suddenly, he looked like the towering superstar he really was and Carly felt herself begin to shrink in comparison. *How on earth had she put herself in this situation?*

What had he said about those beautiful women at the airport? *As interchangeable as the tyres I used to get through.*

Was she out of her mind to contemplate having sex with him?

He was staring down at her. He was so close that she could almost feel the warmth of his body and smell the sandalwood of his soap. She was aware that the bed was within touching distance and she felt torn now—wanting him to reach out for her and terrified of making a fool of herself if he did.

His voice was soft. 'Can't what?'

She bit her lip. 'Can't go through with this.'

'Lesson number one: expressing doubt is not the most flattering way to greet your prospective lover. And neither is standing there with a look of horror on your face.'

'Luis, I'm serious.'

'Relax,' he said. 'And let me look at you.'

She lifted a self-conscious hand towards her collar as his gaze roved over her. The pink T-shirt was new and the plain denim skirt made her hips look less curvy than usual, but even so... 'I've got nothing particularly fancy to wear. And anyway, I certainly wasn't anticipating *this.*'

'But that's what makes you completely lovely,' he said unexpectedly. 'Your lack of calculation and your absence of expectation. Your naturalness is refreshing.'

She stared at him suspiciously. 'I thought you didn't like what I wore?'

He shrugged. 'I don't, particularly. You certainly don't make the best of yourself, but your simplicity has an appeal all of its own. Even the most hardened cynic can have his head turned by a pair of shining eyes and the glow of healthy skin. And at last you are showcasing one of your most beautiful assets.' He lifted a handful of hair and let it fall down around her shoulders. 'Your hair is the stuff of male fantasy. And right now, you are the stuff of *my* fantasy.'

'Luis,' she said breathlessly, realising that some of the tension had left her, only to be replaced by a new and very different kind of tension, and she saw from the darkening of his eyes that he felt it, too.

He moved his hands to her waist and pulled her close and her heart began thumping dangerously as she felt the warmth of his body against hers.

'Carly,' he said softly. 'Sweet, unexpected Carly.'

She didn't say anything and part of him was glad, because for the first time Luis felt the whisper of doubt, and maybe her words might have compounded that doubt. He saw the way she looked at him—all darkened eyes and parted lips. All innocence and wonder. And as he moved closer he was overcome by a wave of lust far sweeter than he had anticipated, and hot on its heels came the dark stir of his conscience.

His mouth tightened.

He must not hurt her.

He would not hurt her.

'Come here,' he said. He cupped her face with both his hands and slowly brought his head down as he began to kiss her.

At first, he kept it light and teasing—a touch of the lips so fleeting that it barely made contact, though he could taste the subtle flavour of her toothpaste and, for some reason, that drove him crazy. And then he deepened the kiss, flickering his tongue inside her mouth as he began to explore her fully clothed body, and she came to life beneath his touch.

It was the most instant and mind-blowing transformation he had ever encountered. Suddenly, she was all fire. The hands which had been lying inert on his shoulders now moved to curl possessively around his neck as he pulled her even closer.

She kissed him with a passion which took him by surprise. He groaned as she tangled her fingers in his hair and melded her pelvis against his. Her lack of guile and experience was making him feel... Luis heard the roar of his own blood. He wasn't sure *how* it was making him feel. Only that, for all his words about wanting a seasoned seduction, he was suddenly peeling off her T-shirt with the same kind of hunger as a hormonally charged teenager. Maybe even more. Because at seventeen everything had been out there waiting for him. Back then he had been completely entranced by women and yet to discover just how devious they could be. He soon found out that what you saw was never the truth. That thick cascades of hair were usually as false as the stories they spun you. That breasts this large usually owed more to the skill of a plastic surgeon, than to nature.

But not with Carly. He swallowed. God, no. Carly seemed...*real.*

He unclipped her bra and drew back as her breasts tumbled out—the fleshy mounds pale and her nipples the colour of cappuccino. She went to cover them up with her hands but he halted her.

'What are you doing?'

'I know they're too big,' she said.

'Are you kidding?' He smiled. 'They are perfect. Your nipples are exactly the right size for a man's mouth. Shall I show you how well they would fit into mine?'

It pleased him that she blushed as she let him remove her hands, leaving those caramel-coloured circles bare to his gaze. He saw her eyelids flicker as if she was fighting something inside her and then they closed as he bent to lick his tongue over one.

'Luis,' she moaned.

But now he said nothing; his teasing dialogue forgotten. In truth, he was in no fit state to talk. He felt himself grow harder as he sucked at her nipples and teased them with his teeth until she was making wild gulping little sounds at the back of her throat. Her denim skirt was restricting and it was with unfamiliar difficulty that he tugged it down over her hips and thighs, before it pooled at her feet. And when at last he put his hand between her legs her panties were very wet.

Gently rubbing at the moist panel of fabric, he carefully pushed her down on the bed and then drew away from her.

'Stay right there,' he commanded unsteadily.

Her voice trembled. 'You think I'm in any fit state to go anywhere?'

'You are a woman who constantly surprises me,' he said drily. 'So I wouldn't care to make a wager on that.'

Carly watched as he tugged the clothes from his body with an impatience which seemed charged with extra urgency, though his hand was completely steady as he placed a condom on the locker beside her phone.

She had expected to be daunted by the sight of seeing Luis completely naked and aroused and ready to make love, but she wasn't. The truth of it was that her starved and eager body felt nothing but *relief* as he finally dropped his boxer shorts to the floor and joined her on the bed. She could feel the rough hair on his chest squishing against her bare breasts as he kissed her. His hand skated down to her hips, his fingers slipping beneath the elastic of her panties, before sliding them down over her knees.

He kissed her breasts and he kissed her belly. He touched her intimately until she was writhing with pleasure and a hunger which had become all-consuming. Suddenly, she didn't feel like Carly any more—she felt like… Her head tipped back. She felt like a woman. A *real* woman, and suddenly the inequality of their experience didn't matter. Greedily, her fingers explored his body in a way she'd wanted to do for so long. So very long. She touched the angled bones and honed muscle. She skated her fingers over the silken surface of his skin and then she dragged her lips from his, grazing them along his jaw, before finding the warmth of his ear.

'Please,' she whispered, barely conscious of what it was she was asking for.

'Please, what?' he murmured, his fingers moving down to part her moist labia so that she jerked with pleasure. 'This?'

She supposed she must have nodded or said something, or maybe it was obvious just from the eager way she clung to him how much she wanted him. She felt him reach out for the condom and the tearing open of the foiled package sounded unnaturally loud to her highly sensitised ears. She knew a moment of trepidation as she felt him prepare himself, but then he was moving over her and she could feel the engorged tip of him pressing against her.

She looked up into his face and the weirdest thing was that the look which passed between them seemed like the most intimate thing which had happened so far.

'Luis,' she whispered.

'It may…hurt a little,' he said, his voice doing that soft and unsteady thing all over again. 'I don't know. I'll do my best to make sure it doesn't.'

And then he was easing himself into her. Slowly. Deliciously. Filling her as if her body had been nothing but an empty space, just waiting for him to fill it. It didn't hurt like the books and the stories sometimes said it did. There was a moment of acute discomfort—but then it was gone. And that was the moment when pleasure began to swamp out trepidation and doubt and every other negative feeling and replaced them all with satisfaction, and joy.

He moved inside her. He coaxed her and teased her. He made anything seem possible. At first she thought the shimmering of something hovering on the edge of her understanding was a flicker of something impossible. But when it happened again she began to stiffen with fear that she might somehow miss it. Like closing your eyes when you were looking at a rainbow and when you opened them again it was gone.

'Relax, *querida*,' he murmured as he made another deep thrust inside her.

Perhaps it was the '*querida*' which took the fantasy one stage further, which made her believe that anything *was* possible. She was poised on the brink of something magical, reaching out for something which kept slipping beyond her reach...and then suddenly it was happening. Her body was contracting and it was all about everlasting rainbows as Luis tipped his head back and gave a helpless kind of groan.

And Carly's body seemed to splinter into a million beautiful pieces.

CHAPTER EIGHT

CARLY COULDN'T SLEEP, and in the end she gave up trying.

Slowly, she got out of a bed which was still rumpled and scented with the unfamiliar smell of sex. Looking down, she saw the indentation of the second pillow; tangible evidence that for the first time in her life she had not slept alone, and she felt her skin shivering with pleasure as she remembered.

She had slept with Luis.

She had given her virginity to the Argentinian playboy with an eagerness which was making her blush even now.

Scooping mussed hair back from her face, she laid her palms over her hot cheeks. Because not very much sleeping had taken place, had it? It had been one long night of discovery.

She swallowed, remembering how nervous she'd been. How she'd been fretting and pacing in her bedroom, too scared to go down to supper. But somehow he had made it all okay. He had come to her room and started kissing her and, instead of being some big deal, it had just seemed to *happen*. As if it was all perfectly natural and normal, just as he'd said it should be. She had made love with Luis Martinez and he seemed to have enjoyed it just as much as she had done.

Supper had been forgotten and it had been almost ten when he had pulled on his jeans and brought back some of the neglected food from the terrace. They had eaten grapes and slithers of mountain cheese in bed, and he had opened a bottle of wine called Petrus and given a small smile when she had pronounced it 'really nice'.

And he had gone to his own room just as dawn had begun to filter through the sky in streaks of red and gold. Bending his dark head, he had kissed her and told her it would probably be easier if he wasn't there in the morning.

He was right about that, too. She knew that. It was nothing but stupidity which made her wish that he'd stayed all night; a flicker of yearning which she knew was dangerous and pointless. So she forced herself to concentrate on the practical instead, which she was good at. She told herself that no way would he want his staff to know how he'd spent the previous evening and she couldn't think of anything worse than Simone discovering him leaving her bedroom, looking tousled and unshaven. Something like that would only make her own position more difficult...though she hadn't actually given a lot of thought as to what was going to happen now.

Now that Luis had taken her as his lover.

Padding barefooted into the bathroom, she pulled on the fluffy robe which was hanging on the back of the door and knotted it tightly at her waist. She certainly wasn't going to do the whole guilt trip—not with herself and not with him. Even if it never happened again, she would always be grateful for the way he'd made her feel. He had set her free from the past. He'd made her realise that she was capable of experiencing the same kind of pleasure as anyone else.

What had he said to her before it had all happened? The one phrase which had stuck out in her mind.

I like your clear-headed way of thinking.

She knew why he'd said that. Because she'd told him she wasn't hung up on love, or marriage. Because she'd convinced him that she was able to regard this sexual experience with complete objectivity.

So why did she suddenly want to hug her arms around herself and dance around the room, while music played loudly inside her head?

The sun was higher now, turning the sea a deep shade of rose, and when she walked out onto the terrace the air felt still and clear. The house was quiet but her head and body were buzzing and for once the thought of losing herself in a few pages of quantum physics didn't appeal. She would catch up on her emails, then see what the day would bring. And if Luis had decided that one night was enough—well, she would have to accept it like a grown-up.

She logged onto her email account and found three messages from her sister. The first was titled Where are u? The second consisted of nothing but a long row of question marks, and the third announced, rather more dramatically, WHAT THE HELL IS HAPPENING?

Carly clicked onto this one first, but unusually the email wasn't peppered with smiley faces or descriptions of her sister's latest modelling jobs. For once, the message was all about Carly.

Saw a photo of your boss at Nice airport and it looked like YOU in the background. I said to Mum that nobody else would wear a T-shirt like that in the Côte d'Azur!!! Are you really in the south of France with Luis Martinez—and if so what the hell is going on?????

Carly smiled. She wondered how Bella would react if she told her the unbelievable truth. *Yes, I am here with Luis. In fact, I told him about my past and he's decided to teach me everything he knows about sex, which is fairly comprehensive as I'm sure you can guess.* Imagine drafting *that* into an email!

She clicked to reply.

Yes, it's true. I've been helping Luis with his rehab after his accident, and he decided it would be preferable if he got better in the sunshine. It's absolutely gorgeous here. Aren't I lucky? Love, Carly xxx

She hit the send button just as someone tapped on the door, but before she had a chance to answer—it opened quietly and Luis walked into the room. He was freshly shaved and his black eyes were alive with vitality and a spark of something else which already she recognised as desire.

'Hello,' he said softly as he closed the door behind him.

Carly's hand crept up to her throat as she realised that the white bathrobe was deeply unflattering and probably added at least ten extra pounds to her frame. 'I thought you'd decided that it was better not to risk being seen here.'

'Maybe I've changed my mind.'

'I haven't even brushed my teeth.'

'Then go and brush them now,' he instructed silkily. 'Because I like the taste of your toothpaste.'

She escaped into the bathroom and when she returned, it was to discover that Luis had dropped his clothes on the floor and was in her bed—completely naked amid the still-rumpled sheets.

'What are you doing?'

'Isn't it obvious?'

'But...what about the staff?'

'What about them? The only member of my staff I'm interested in is standing right in front of me, wearing far too many clothes.' He patted the empty space beside him. 'So come over here, *querida*, before I grow too impatient.'

Carly swallowed down the sudden apprehension which had risen in her throat. It would probably be better to resist him, when even now the gardeners would be arriving and the chef sending his assistant down to the markets in Nice to buy fresh fish and vegetables for the day. To tell him that this was an extremely unwise move and surely they could arrange a rather more discreet meeting later.

It would be much better.

So why was she walking towards the bed and pulling back the sheets?

And why was Luis shaking his head like that?

'No. Not yet. Lose the robe,' he instructed silkily. 'And don't tell me you're shy, not now, when I happen to know more about your body than any man on the planet.'

It was difficult to act nonchalantly when the harsh light of day was showing no mercy to her too-generous curves, but Carly did her best. 'I'm glad to see that nothing ever manages to deflate your ego,' she said, unknotting the robe and letting it fall to the floor, before quickly sliding between the sheets and colliding with his warm, hard body.

'Not just my ego,' he said as he guided her

hand to his groin and bent his head to kiss her. 'Mmm. Toothpaste.'

He kissed her until she relaxed. Until her body had begun to call out to her with a hunger which was already familiar and impossible to ignore. And again, Carly was lost as her whole world became centred on what he was doing to her.

She closed her eyes as he cupped her breasts, his palms rolling rhythmically over her peaking nipples. She squirmed with pleasure as he moved over her, parting her thighs and positioning himself there. She gasped as he entered her with one long, slow thrust, her head tipping back as he began to move inside her. Her fingertips roved over his skin, greedily exploring all the different textures, from the hard, hair-roughened thighs to the silken expanse of his broad back.

She wanted to revel in this feeling of intimacy and pleasure, but her orgasm rushed upon her with the speed and power of a freight train crashing over eggshells. She heard him cry out almost immediately, that strangely vulnerable moan he made as he shuddered into stillness inside her. She cradled her arms tightly around him and snuggled up close, her head resting comfortably on his shoulder.

And then she fell asleep.

When she awoke he had gone, just as he'd done last night, and when she appeared at the breakfast table, Simone informed her that Monsieur Martinez had gone into Nice on business and she didn't know when he'd be back.

The morning seemed to pass like an eternity and Carly found it impossible to concentrate on anything. He didn't return until late in the afternoon and by the time he came to her room to find her, she was convinced he was regretting what had happened.

'Where have you been?' she blurted out, before she could stop herself.

He raised his eyebrows.

'I'm sorry. It's none of my business.'

He gave a short laugh as he pulled her into his arms. 'I needed space, and I needed to do some business without any distractions. But now I find I'm in the mood for distraction.'

He pushed her down onto the bed, removing her clothes with almost clinical efficiency, and as Carly looked into the hungry gleam of his black eyes she guessed that this was a demonstration that sex could be fast and furious, too.

Afterwards, she lay there feeling slightly dazed, drawing little circles on his skin and realising that he knew far more about her than she did about him. And in her dreamy post-orgasmic state, she felt she could ask him anything.

'Luis?'

'Mmm?'

She turned onto her side, propping herself up on her elbow so that spills of hair fell down over her shoulders and covered her breasts. 'Have you never wanted children of your own?'

His mouth tightened as he brushed away the curtain of hair to expose her nipple. 'Another word of advice,' he drawled. 'As a post-coital topic, fatherhood isn't really a winner. Be warned, any dreamy little references to babies is likely to send any future lovers running off into the sunset. They might worry that you're starting to fall in love with them.'

She ignored the stab of disappointment that he seemed totally without sexual jealousy; she didn't think *she* could have been quite so casual about any future lovers he might have. But she stuck to her guns. To consider the question logically, as she had been taught. 'You think a question about children automatically means I'm falling in love with you?'

'I know the signs,' he drawled.

'Well, in my case you are misreading them,' she said coolly. 'I'm interested purely from a human interest point of view. Most men want to recreate—it's in their DNA. Continuation of the human race, that sort of thing. You've built up a massive empire, you're a millionaire many times over, surely you want your own flesh and blood to inherit all that?'

Luis rolled onto his back and stared up at the ceiling. It was a topic he usually snapped the lid on—fast. He didn't like women probing and it bored him when they searched for feelings which weren't there. He wondered why was she was spoiling things by asking him this kind of question.

Yet Carly wasn't looking for the kinds of things which most women wanted, was she? A question he'd normally consider loaded, and which he would deflect with ease, sounded different when it came from her. With Carly, he had laid out all his ground rules from the start. She knew what he would or wouldn't tolerate. She was ambitious for a career, not marriage, and perhaps that was why he felt relaxed enough to answer her question.

'I think the human race will survive very well without any miniature versions of Luis Martinez,' he said drily.

'Any particular reason?'

'I can see that you're going to make a very good doctor.' He turned his head to meet her eyes. 'Since you're very persistent with your questions.'

'You're stalling.'

'So I am.' His eyes gleamed. 'What do you want to know?'

'Oh, I don't know. About your life. Where you grew up. Why you're so adamant you don't want children.'

He linked his fingers together and put them behind his head, allowing a slow stream of memories to pass through his mind. 'I grew up on a big ranch outside Buenos Aires,' he said. 'Where we farmed cattle in great rolling sweeps of land with the biggest skies you ever saw.'

She wriggled a little closer. 'We?'

'Me, my mother and my father. We were quite unusual in that there weren't loads of children running around. But I guess that made us especially close as a family, and my parents...' He shrugged. 'Well, they adored me, I guess. The farm was hugely profitable, my father had business interests in the city which were equally successful...'

'So everything was lovely?' she prompted as his voice faded away.

'For a while.' He looked at her and when he

spoke again his voice had grown hard. 'My mother had a friend called Amelita, and she and her husband had a son about my age. Vicente was like the brother I'd never had, and the two families used to do everything together. We skied in the winter and hit the beaches in the summer. We ate Christmas dinner around the same table. We were all like one great big unit.'

He paused, not sure why he was telling her all this. Not sure that he should. Was it because she had shared her secrets with him and something was telling him that he needed to redress the balance? Or because he suspected that she was insistent enough to keep probing if he didn't?

'Go on,' she said.

He stroked her hair. 'I developed a love of speed early on and my father built a small go-kart circuit on our property for me to practise on, which was pretty innovative at the time. Vicente and I spent hours bombing around that dusty trail. Then at sixteen, I moved away to the San Luis province so that I could use the famous Potrero de los Funes track. I didn't come home that often, but when I did, things seemed different. I thought that my father and Amelita had grown…close. Closer than was right. I used to see the way she looked at him. The way she dressed around him. For a while I managed to convince myself that I must be mistaken, because I *wanted* to be mistaken. And she was my mother's best friend.'

He swallowed. His own sexual experience had been at a fledgling stage—he was barely out of single figures himself at that time. But he had been hit on often enough to realise that his mother's best friend really was coming onto his father. He remembered trying to talk to him about it and being shocked by the old man's sudden spurt of rage; his gritted threat to punch his only son. He had allowed himself to be placated by the furious denials which had followed, because hadn't it been easier that way, even if deep down he had known the words to be lies?

'And then one afternoon I rose early from my siesta,' he said slowly. 'The day was so still and so hot that I felt I could hardly breathe. I walked outside, seeking the shade of the trees, but it was no better there. There was no relief to be found anywhere. And then I heard a sound, something which seemed out of place in my home. I found myself walking towards the summer house and that is where I found them. My father and Amelita...'

Carly's hand flew over her mouth so that her words came out muffled. 'And were they...?'

'Not quite,' he said, repressing a painful shudder of recall. 'Amelita was in the middle of some kind of tacky striptease at the time, while my father...' His voice shook with rage. 'And all this while my mother slept in the house nearby. It was the lack of respect as much as the betrayal which made me want to kill him.'

He stopped speaking and she didn't say anything. She moved her hand to his face to try to comfort him, but he shook it off as if a fly had landed there.

'It all came out, of course. These things always do,' he said. 'I suspect Amelita made sure that it did, since my father was one of the richest men in Argentina. And predictably, it blew everyone's world apart. My mother never really recovered. She felt the sting of the double betrayal, of being cheated on not just by her husband, but by her best friend, too. She moved out of the ranch and bought a place in the city, but she stopped eating. Stopped caring, really. She used to stay in her rooms, afraid to leave, haunted by the fact that people would be looking at her and mocking her. Didn't matter what I did or what anyone said, she refused to listen, and she died just three years later.'

'Oh, Luis. I'm so sorry,' she whispered.

He shook his head as he tried to hold back the tide of dark emotion which he had battened down for so long. But for once in his life, it kept on coming and some instinct told him that maybe it was better this way. He had never told anyone, and if he told someone who ultimately didn't matter, then couldn't he loosen some of his own dark chains? Because one thing he knew was that Carly would never go anywhere with this. He could see the makings of the doctor in her already, not just in her firm but ultimately gentle care of him, but in a moral compass, which was rare. She would not need to swear the Hippocratic oath to have her discretion guaranteed.

'You want to hear the rest?' he questioned bitterly. 'Because it doesn't make for a particularly happy bedtime story.'

'I want to hear it,' she said.

'The husband of my father's mistress also felt humiliated by the public laughing stock he'd become, but he sought a different remedy than the self-imposed isolation of my mother. He took what he thought was the only honourable way out. He put a revolver to his head and blew his brains out. It was Vicente who found him.'

She drew in a deep, shuddering breath. 'Oh, Luis.'

He stared up at the ceiling again. 'So there you have it. Now do you see why I don't believe in family life and happy ever after, Carly?'

There was a pause. He could almost hear her thinking aloud as she sifted through all the possible words and tried to find the right ones to say. Except that there were no right words. He knew that.

'Not...really,' she said tentatively. 'I mean—those were terrible things which happened, but they weren't really anything to do with you, were they? None of that was your fault. Just because of the way your father behaved, doesn't automatically follow that you would do the same. Infidelity and betrayal aren't hereditary, you know.'

He turned to look at her again. He could see empathy clouding her eyes and he couldn't help admire her kindness, as well as her perception. Because Carly was clever, he realised. Clever enough to realise that there was more.

'But I've lived a life on the racing circuit,' he said simply. 'And I've seen what it does to men—especially to champions.'

'What do you mean?'

He shrugged. 'There are characteristics which make men like me succeed. We're driven—literally—by the desire to win. We spend years in pursuit of the elusive perfect lap and when we achieve it we want to repeat it, over and over again. There aren't many of us at the top, but when you get there you realise that it is both a seductive and a dangerous place to be. People revere you. They want a piece of you. Especially women.'

'Women who are *"as interchangeable as the tyres I used to get through"*?' she quoted quietly.

'Exactamente.' His face tightened. 'I have seen the strongest marriages break down under the strain of all the temptations the sport has to offer. When the adrenaline is flowing and some sexy little creature puts on a skirt the size of a handkerchief and presses her breasts against your windshield, most men can't say no. Most are arrogant enough to feel they *don't have to* say no.'

'So.' She sat up, folding her arms across her naked breasts. 'What you're really saying is that world champions get given so much forbidden fruit, that they find it impossible to exist on normal fare like most normal people?'

He shrugged. 'If you like.'

'But you no longer race for a living, Luis,' she said. 'So how does that even apply?'

'My father wasn't a racer,' he said stonily. 'He was a farmer who'd been married for twenty-one years. Who used to tell me that my mother was his soulmate.'

'So what you're really saying is that you think men generally are incapable of fidelity?'

'That's one way of looking at it,' he said slowly. 'Yes. I think that's right.'

'So men really are the weaker sex?'

'Or the more realistic?' he countered coolly. 'How can two people possibly make promises of fidelity to each other, when they have no guarantee of keeping them?'

Carly didn't respond. His words had made her heart sink, even though she knew she had no right to be hurt by them. He had never promised her anything other than what he'd just given her, had he? In fact, he had explicitly warned her off the very things he had just been talking about.

She pushed back the sheet and got out of bed. 'I need to use the bathroom,' she said.

She walked across the bedroom and closed the bathroom door behind her, though maybe you were supposed to leave it open in circumstances like these? She realised what a novice she still was and how little she knew about how to interact with a man on such an intimate basis. She told herself that she couldn't complain about his honesty, just because he was telling her something she didn't want to hear. She had to accept this on the terms he had offered her, or she would end up getting her heart broken.

She flicked cold water over her face and practised a few convincing-looking smiles in the mirror so that when she walked back into the bedroom she felt almost calm. At least, until she saw him sitting propped up against the bank of snowy pillows, looking very dark and rugged.

His black eyes seemed to pierce through her still-tender skin. 'Would you like to go out for lunch tomorrow?' he questioned.

'Lunch?' She blinked, because she had assumed that they would assume their normal boss/employee relationship during daylight hours. She had thought that they would be together only in bed. 'You mean—not here?'

He gave the faint flicker of a smile, as if her lack of imagination had amused him. 'No, not here. There is a whole beautiful coastline out there, *querida*—with some of the most famous restaurants in the world just waiting to be eaten in. There are beaches and mountains and tiny villages which are like stepping back in time. And since this is your first visit to France, I think it's time I showed you some of them.'

'But…I thought you'd decided it was best if we weren't seen together?'

'And maybe I've changed my mind.' His mouth tightened. 'I don't live my life trying to please other people, and neither should you.'

CHAPTER NINE

HE TOOK HER to Juan-les-Pins, to a restaurant on a beach, where he was recognised immediately. But Carly was still too busy thinking about what he'd told her to take much notice of the heads turning to watch them as they walked over the sand-covered boards to a table which looked directly over the lapping blue waves. She thought about his sad upbringing and the conclusions he'd drawn. Conclusions which had only been compounded by his championship status in the glamorous sport of motor racing.

He didn't think that men were capable of fidelity.

It had been a bald statement to make to someone you'd only just seduced and the message had been plain, even for someone as naïve as her. He was warning her off. Telling her to keep this bizarre liaison in the right place and not start building any fantasies. Because he wasn't stupid. He must guess that being sexually awoken by a man like him would be powerful enough to turn the head of any woman, no matter how much she protested that she wasn't looking for love or marriage.

They ordered shellfish salads, and iced lime juice flavoured with coconut, and Luis devoured his food with a voracious appetite before noticing that she wasn't doing the same. He put his fork down and looked at her, dark eyebrows disappearing into the tangle of his dark hair.

'Lobster not to your satisfaction?'

She prodded at the pink flesh with her fork and forced a smile. 'The lobster's lovely.'

'Is that why you're not eating any of it? Or is it because you're upset about what I told you yesterday?'

'I'm not *upset*. I'm grateful you felt you could be so honest with me. I'm just feeling a bit...'

He put his glass down. 'A bit what?'

She shrugged. 'Nothing.'

'Tell me.'

'Oh, I don't know. Overwhelmed, I guess.' Her gaze shot around at the tables, which all seemed to contain at least one female who looked as if she'd be at home on a catwalk. 'All the women here look amazing. As if they've spent the entire morning getting ready to have lunch in a chic restaurant, while I—'

'Look like someone who has spent the morning being ravished by a man who can't seem to keep his hands off her? Who is growing hard just by looking at her.'

'Luis,' she said faintly, her breath catching in her throat, because when he looked at her that way she just wanted to lean across the table and kiss him.

'Don't you think that any of them would prefer to be in your shoes?' His gaze dropped to floor level and the hint of a smile curved his lips. 'Or flip-flops, in this case.'

'Which were never bought with the intention of being worn in some ultra-smart restaurant on the Côte d'Azur.'

He glanced up. 'But you don't dress to be seen, do you, Carly? Or to be looked at. You dress to be invisible and to blend into the background. I thought that was the whole point.'

She could hear the white umbrella above them flapping in the light breeze which was coming off the sea. 'And I told you why.'

'But the reason no longer applies, surely? If I've set you free from your hang-ups about sex, then doesn't it follow that you might be a little more experimental about what you wear?'

'You think I look awful,' she said, in a wooden voice.

'I think those pale shades you like don't do you any favours. Your colouring is so fair that you need something more dramatic to set that off. If you don't like your appearance, then change it, but don't keep doing nothing and then complaining about it, because it's boring.' He leaned back in his chair and subjected her to a cool look. 'And there's no need to look at me quite so reproachfully. You *did* ask.'

'And you certainly didn't p-pull any punches in telling me,' she said.

'What would be the point of that? We're back to the whole question of honesty again.' He shrugged. 'Maybe it's time you stopped hiding some of your more spectacular assets and tried something new. So grab your bag.' He lifted his hand and signalled to the waiter for the check. 'I'm taking you shopping.'

'I don't like shopping.'

'You will. Like eating avocado—it's a taste which can easily be acquired.' His black eyes gleamed. 'So come quietly, *querida*, because I am still not fit enough to put you over my shoulder and carry you.'

Carly bit back a smile. When he looked at her that way, she felt powerless to do anything but agree. She didn't feel like herself any more; she had become one of those women starring in a rom-com, their lives transformed by a gorgeous man with a big wallet and a lot of attitude.

Clamping her hands down over her hair, they sped along the Croisette in Cannes in his open-top car before coming to a halt outside a screamingly smart boutique, where a burly man in uniform took Luis's car keys and went off to park for him.

But Carly's mood evaporated when she peered through the plate-glass windows at the glamorous sales assistants who were grouped around inside.

'I can't,' she whispered. 'I can't go in there.'

'I thought we'd decided to dispense with the self-deprecation?' he drawled. 'You can do anything you want. Starting right now.' He laced his fingers in hers. 'Come.'

Carly felt faint. He was holding her hand in public! He was walking inside as if he owned the place and telling one of the sales assistant that he wanted to see her in 'hot' colours.

'Scarlet,' he said. 'And definitely flame. And I think we might try yellow, too.'

Slipping into seamless French, he spoke animatedly to the woman, using his hands to draw curving shapes of a voluptuous body in the air. They were taken to a private area at the back

of the store, where he showed no embarrassment about running his fingertips along a line
of frothy lace bras, or deliberating between the
virtues of the thong versus the camiknicker.

Carly's throat had grown dry with nerves.
She felt big and ungainly, like a giant in a land
of tiny people. She wanted to tell him she'd
changed her mind, until she remembered that
it hadn't actually been her who had made it
up in the first place. It had been Luis who had
taken command of the afternoon, overriding
all her objections and deciding what needed to
be done. And judging by his relaxed attitude
as he sat on one of the velvet sofas, sipping a
tiny cup of espresso, this wasn't the first time
he'd adopted this particular role. Maybe it was
just a rite of passage for all the women who
shared his bed. Though surely the usual rangy
supermodel would do more justice to one of the
delicate pieces of underwear which had been
brought to the cubicle for her to try?

But to Carly's surprise, the wispy bra was
deceptively supportive and the camiknickers

transformed her rounded hips into an area of her body which suddenly looked glossy, and… inviting.

When she pulled on a yellow and white polka-dot dress, with its full skirt and shiny patent belt, she barely recognised the reflection which gazed back from the mirror, but even the sales assistant gave her a wide beam of approval.

'*Mais, elle est jolie,*' she said, on a note of surprise.

Luis gave a slow smile as Carly stood in front of him. 'Very pretty,' he agreed, picking up a straw sun hat with a yellow ribbon on—his black eyes piercing into her as he placed it carefully on her head. 'Now are you going to start believing in yourself?'

She could feel the silk next to her skin and the crispness of the petticoat beneath the fifties-style dress and, almost shyly, she nodded.

He smiled, his gaze alighting on a stick-like mannequin clutching a plastic bucket and spade at the far end of the store. 'I think we'll take a look at some bikinis while we're here.'

Soon they were laden down with glossy carrier bags, tied with bright pink ribbons, and Carly was persuaded to keep on the yellow dress and the matching espadrilles.

'You've bought me far too much,' she whispered, her heart pounding as Luis cupped her face in his hands, causing the sun hat to wobble precariously.

'That's for me to do and for you to accept. And now I'm going to take you home and show you something which is vital to the repertoire of any lover,' he said, brushing his lips over hers in a grazing kiss.

Carly was back on that same dangerous high as they sped along the mountain road. She kept trying to tell herself that none of this had any real substance, no matter how wonderful it felt. But her heart was stubbornly refusing to listen to what her head was telling her. She had told him she wasn't looking for the things which most women wanted—that her desire for love and marriage had been eclipsed by her ambition to be a doctor. But suddenly she was discovering that falling in love with Luis would be as easy as falling off a chair.

He took her straight to his bedroom when they got back, but she barely had time to register that this was the first time she'd ever been in his room because he was closing the door and walking towards her, with a look of fierce intent on his face.

His eyes were glittering as he began to peel off her yellow dress before carefully draping it over the back of a chair. Beneath it she was wearing some of the new lingerie he'd chosen and she saw his eyes narrow as he ran his gaze over her.

'*Perfecta,*' he said softly.

'I'm not perfect,' she said, until she saw the expression on his face. 'Th-thank you.'

'That's better.' He gave a small nod of approval as he cupped the embroidered swell of her breast. 'Because right now, you are completely perfect to me.'

Carly would have defied a marble statue not to have responded to that statement. She tried to play down its significance as he pushed her onto the silken rug and took off her new camiknickers, before putting his head between her thighs. She stiffened at the shock of the sudden warm intimacy of his tongue licking against her moist flesh. Her fingers started tugging at the wayward waves of his hair so that he lifted his head, his dark eyes gleaming as they surveyed her.

'Luis?' she said uncertainly.

'You just have to relax,' he said. 'I'm not going to hurt you.'

Wasn't he? She closed her eyes. She suspected he was going to do exactly that. Because there were different kinds of hurt, weren't there? She'd learnt in biology that the human heart was vulnerable in so many ways.

But her mind emptied as his tongue began to explore her. She clung to him as he whispered soft incitements in Spanish. And after she had sobbed out a powerful orgasm which left her dazed and shaking, she wondered how she was going to live without this kind of pleasure.

Or live without him.

She could taste the unfamiliar flavour of sex on his mouth as he slid up to kiss her.

'Unzip me,' he said.

She swallowed. 'Are you going to corrupt me even more?'

'I'm going to try.'

He taught her how to suck him. He showed her how to pleasure herself, while he watched. He took her to Monaco and Antibes and Saint-Paul-de-Vence, where they ate lunch in a famous restaurant, where paintings by Picasso and Miro hung on the walls. They ate *plateau de fruits de mer* in Nice and drank champagne in a little place called Plan-du-Var, high up in the mountains. Back at his luxury villa he would strip off her clothes with hungry hands and their sex would have a hot, hard urgency. And when she had gasped out yet another orgasm, he would stroke her skin and murmur that her body was everything a woman's body should be. By the end of that week, Carly was reeling—her senses so exquisitely stimulated that she could barely eat or sleep.

And all she could think about was Luis.

It was as if he had entered her bloodstream like a powerful drug. Suddenly, she began to understand something about the nature of addiction. You tried something which you knew was bad for you, and suddenly you were hooked. Hooked on a feeling which even a novice could recognise as love.

But none of this was real. That was what she kept bringing it back to. It was a brief fairy tale which was bound to end. Her feelings weren't real and neither was this situation. Seduced by his skill as a lover, she had found it easy to forget she was also Luis's employee. But she was. Nothing had really changed and now she was wondering what was going to happen when they left here.

'You've been very quiet,' he observed late one afternoon as they lay beside the pool and she tried, unsuccessfully, to read.

'I'm just sleepy.'

'Don't be evasive, Carly,' he said softly. 'I thought we had agreed to be honest with each other.'

She laid the book down on her stomach, her heart clenching as she looked at him. The growing ache inside her was making her realise she couldn't carry on like this. She couldn't keep burying her head in the sand and pretending the future wasn't out there. She couldn't keep pretending that she didn't care for him, because she did. 'I've been thinking.'

'About what?'

'Well, a couple of things really.' For a moment the world seemed to hold its breath and everything around her seemed to be green and blue and beautiful. The flickering gleam of sunlight danced on the pool and the sky was as blue as those rain-smashed delphiniums she'd seen in the garden back in England. She didn't ever want to leave here, but some day soon she was going to have to. Because they were living in a protected bubble and sooner or later the bubble was going to burst. 'About what's going to happen when we go back to England.'

Luis tipped his sun hat forward, so that the shadow of the brim fell over his eyes, because somehow it was easier to know that his face was in darkness. He thought about her question and how he was going to answer it. She was only saying what had been on his mind for days, and he knew he couldn't keep ignoring his commitments elsewhere. He had a doctor's appointment in London next week and a growing stack of engagements, which he couldn't put off any longer. He had meetings in Dublin and Buenos Aires and was due to make a visit to Uruguay, to oversee the second stage of his beachside development.

But this wasn't just about the logistics of his life; it was about how he was going to deal with a situation he had created. How he was going to extricate himself from it, with as little angst as possible.

He sighed. He liked Carly. He liked her a lot, but the longer this went on, the greater the likelihood that she would get hurt, because that was what he did to women. That was his *process*. And he didn't want to hurt her. He didn't want tears or recriminations. He didn't want her to degrade herself by trying to hold onto what they could never have. He wanted her to go away and be the fantastic doctor he knew she could be.

'I don't think that's going to be a problem,' he said.

'Maybe not. But we still have to face facts, don't we, Luis? There's no point pretending that nothing's happened, is there?'

Beneath the shadowed brim of his hat, Luis frowned. What did she think had *happened*? They'd had sex. She had been unfulfilled and uptight and crying out for some kind of affection. And he had given it to her. He had set her free. His mouth hardened. *That had been the deal*.

He looked at her, at the zingy new orange and cerise bikini which moulded itself to her magnificent curves. She'd left her hair loose, the way he liked it, and her skin had now turned a deep, caramel colour. He'd done her a favour. And he would do her an even bigger one by setting her free.

'I don't think it will be a problem,' he said coolly. 'In fact, I'm planning on leaving almost as soon as we get back to England. I have a number of global projects which will keep me occupied for most of the winter. We'll hardly see one another, probably not until the spring.'

'Oh. Oh, right.'

There was no disguising her shock or her disappointment. He could see she was doing her best to smile, but he knew enough about women to realise that behind her dark glasses those iced-tea eyes would be blinking away the first prick of tears. Because he made women cry, didn't he? That was something else he was good at. He made them long for something he was incapable of giving them. He felt a twist of something which felt like regret, but it was gone in an instant.

'And you'll soon be going off to med school, won't you? You're going to be a doctor. The best doctor in the world.'

Carly was about to tell him that it would be at least a year before she could afford to do that. Because even with the bonus he was paying her, she still needed to pay her rent and feed herself through six long years of study. For someone who hadn't done any formal education for such a long time, she wanted to give one hundred per cent of herself to her course and not distract herself with part-time jobs.

Until she realised the implications of what he was saying, and all the practical considerations about her future slipped from her mind. She realised what was happening and suddenly she felt sick. Luis was ending it. Now. As clinically as he was able to remove her clothes, he was now taking a scalpel to their relationship. He intended going off round the world and when he returned, they would act as if nothing had happened.

Because nothing had.

They'd had sex, that was all. All it was ever intended to be. Only a fool would imagine that the act of *making* love would make someone *fall* in love.

And she was that fool, wasn't she? That fool who had started looking at him with a warm glow in her heart and stupid little fantasies building in her mind.

She swallowed.

She was only that fool if she let herself be.

Quietly, she closed the pages of her book. 'That's right,' she said, hoping her face didn't betray the pain in her heart. 'I will. The best doctor in the world,' she repeated.

He glanced over at her. 'And what was the second thing?'

She stared at him. 'The second thing?'

'You said you had a couple of things you wanted to talk to me about.'

Had she? Carly blinked and then remembered. In the parallel universe of a few minutes ago when there had still been hope in her heart, she had been about to tackle a few home truths. She had wanted to tell him something she thought he needed to hear, but now she thanked heaven that his words had stopped her in time.

Dimly, she registered the sound of an approaching car in the distance, then the slamming of a door and the clatter of heels. But the momentary intrusion was dwarfed by the cold and tearing pain inside her. There was no going back—or going forward. She and Luis were finished. It was over.

She stared into his face. 'It doesn't matter now,' she said, just as Simone began to walk out from the back of the villa, closely followed by someone with long blonde hair and a tiny denim skirt. Someone who looked oddly familiar but who really shouldn't be here.

Carly blinked. It was weird. Like seeing a double-decker bus in the middle of the desert. They were both things you recognised, just that one of them was in the wrong place.

Simone's face was expressionless as she looked at Carly. 'Your sister has arrived.'

'My sister?' said Carly in confusion, as the blonde in the miniskirt came clattering towards them.

CHAPTER TEN

CARLY SAT BOLT UPRIGHT. 'Bella?' she said, her voice rising in surprise. 'What…what on earth are you doing here?' But deep down, she knew. The reason was fairly obvious and lying sprawled on a sunbed which her sister was now standing beside as she slanted him the widest smile in her repertoire.

'Well.' Bella pushed a spill of platinum hair away from her tanned face. 'You told me you were here in Cap Ferrat and I happened to be in the area—'

'What are you doing in the area?' asked Carly, but Bella was shooting her a furious *don't-ask-me-any-awkward-questions* type of look and years of deferring to her sister's wishes was a hard habit to break, especially when you were already feeling emotionally wobbly. She forced a smile. 'Luis, I'd like you to meet my sister, Bella. Bella, this is Luis Martinez, who is—'

'Ex-champion motor-racer of the world,' purred Bella. 'Yes, I know.'

'Oh, that was a long time ago,' said Luis smoothly. 'Nice to meet you, Bella.'

Bella was staring at him with open admiration as he sat up and pushed back his battered straw hat.

'I hope I'm not intruding,' she said.

'Not at all,' he answered. 'As you can see, your sister and I were just catching the last of the afternoon sun. Would you like some coffee? A drink, perhaps?'

'Ooh, a drink would be wonderful. I've been doing the most horrendous shoot all day and I'm knackered. The photographer has practically had his lens up my bum all day.' She licked her lips. 'I don't suppose you've got any champagne?'

'I think we might be able to find some.' He glanced up at his French housekeeper. 'Simone—I wonder if you'd mind...?'

'*Oui, monsieur,*' said Simone briskly. '*D'accord.*'

'Here, let me get you a chair,' said Luis, and he stood up, a movement which seemed to completely captivate Bella, before walking across to the far side of the terrace towards a small cluster of sunbeds and chairs which stood there.

He was barely out of earshot before Bella turned to Carly, her mouth hanging open in amazement. 'What have you been *doing* to yourself?' she demanded. 'I hardly recognised you! My God—that *bikini*!'

Carly automatically tugged at the frilly bikini bottoms. 'You don't like it?'

'I'm not sure. I don't know if it's really *you*. It certainly looks expensive. What the hell is going on, Carly? How come you're lying out here with Mr Hunky and looking like you were born to it?'

'I've been… I've been helping with Luis's rehabilitation.'

'Is that what you call it? Looked pretty cosy when I arrived, I must say.' Her eyes narrowed. 'You're not…'

On her face was an expression which Carly

had never seen before. Yes, there was amazement and disbelief, but surely that wasn't *jealousy* she could read there?

Bella flicked a strand of platinum hair over her shoulder. 'You're not...*involved* with Luis Martinez, are you?'

Carly looked her straight in the eye. 'Oh, come on, Bella, can you really see someone like Luis bothering with someone like me?'

'No,' said Bella slowly. 'I suppose when you put it like *that*.'

Carly was relieved when Luis arrived back with a chair, though less pleased when Bella removed her high-heeled sandals and proceeded to glug down a glass of the pink champagne, which Simone had just delivered on a tray.

She had forgotten just how glamorous her sister was. How a similar composition of genes could have ended up making someone who looked so different from her. They both had the same amber-coloured eyes, but that was where all similarities ended. Bella's were fringed with heavy dark mascara, which made her look like some kind of startled young deer. And her figure was amazing—nobody could deny that. She had always exercised to within an inch of her life and never ate carbs after six and it showed. Oh, yes. It showed. She could see Luis looking at her, his black eyes narrowed with interest, and Carly felt her heart beginning to sink with the inevitability of it all. Of *course* he would find Bella attractive. Any man would.

She found herself accepting a glass of champagne, even though it was only five in the afternoon, and the bubbles shot straight to her head as she sipped it.

'Carly tells me you're a model, Bella,' said Luis.

'Yes, that's right. Though I still haven't made it *quite* as big as I'd like. At least, not *yet*.' Bella smiled at him from behind her curtain of white-blonde hair. 'I suppose you must know plenty of people in the industry?'

'Some.'

'Perhaps you could introduce me sometime?'

'Perhaps,' he said, non-committally.

Carly sat listening in horrified fascination as Bella ladled out abundant amounts of charm. Was Luis enjoying talking to her sister as much as he appeared to be? She watched him smile as Bella told him a story about the elastic snapping on a pair of bikini bottoms as the photographer homed in for a close-up.

'But about three men dashed over to the rescue with their beach towels!' she said.

'I'll bet they did,' observed Luis.

Carly tried to smile but her mouth seemed stuck in some kind of awful rictus. The alcohol was making her feel *disassociated*…as if she was a spectator in all this and not a participant. She saw Bella glance down surreptitiously at her watch.

'What are you guys doing tonight?' she asked casually. 'You're not free for dinner, by any chance?'

'Sorry.' Luis gave her a quick smile. 'But Carly and I have an engagement which we can't get out of,' he said, without missing a beat.

Carly blinked at him.

They did?

'But we must see you some other time,' he continued. 'Just give us a little more warning next time.' He reached down and picked up his cell phone. 'And in the meantime, I'll have my driver take you back to wherever it is you're going.'

Carly could see the flicker of annoyance on Bella's face, the sulky pout which had made her pretty face crumple. The look which always used to get their mother eating out of her hand, but which seemed to be having absolutely no effect on Luis.

She could feel cold dread building inside her as she wrapped her sarong around her to see Bella out, waiting for the outburst she knew was inevitable—and she wasn't disappointed.

'You do realise you're in danger of making a complete and utter fool of yourself?' hissed Bella as they reached the front door.

'I don't know what you're talking about.'

'Oh, please! It's written all over you, and I'm your sister—I know you better than anyone. It's obvious to me that you're sleeping with him and that you can't tear your eyes away from him. I don't blame you for that—he's pretty amazing—the only surprise is that he's chosen someone like you. I don't want to be cruel, Carly, but you need to hear the facts. And you're heading for a crash if you don't pull yourself together, because it's clear what he's doing.'

Carly felt as if she'd been carved from wood. 'And what's that?'

'He's just playing Pygmalion,' Bella continued, really getting into it now. 'Transforming his mousey little housekeeper into someone who's happy to lie by the swimming pool, bursting out of her bikini. But it's nothing but a *game* for him. Don't you see? He's been bored—and incapacitated—and it's just something to keep himself occupied. He'll drop you just as quickly as he picked you up, and then where will you be?'

There were a million things she could have said in response, but Carly just said the words she knew were expected of her, like someone who was reading from an autocue. *And wasn't Bella only speaking the truth?* 'Thanks for the advice—I'll certainly bear it in mind,' she said. 'Maybe we can meet up when I get back to England?'

Bella stared at her as if waiting for more and when it didn't come, she spoke again. 'And hopefully you'll have seen sense by then.'

'Hopefully.'

Bella shook her head and her blonde hair swayed. 'You're a fool, Carly Conner.'

Carly watched as her sister strutted across the forecourt of the villa and climbed into the car which was waiting. She stood there for a long time after the electronic gates had closed, until there was nothing but a tiny black dot in the distance, spitting up clouds of dust as it drove down the hillside.

She walked slowly back into the house. Now what?

Back to the poolside to finish her glass of champagne and for a conversation she didn't really want to have? Yet deep down she knew she didn't have an alternative. She couldn't avoid the truth for ever.

Luis had obviously been swimming while she'd been saying goodbye to her sister. His dark hair was dripping and his olive skin was sleek with little droplets of water. He walked along the edge of the pool and stretched and suddenly it was as if her vision had cleared. As if she was able to step out of the fog of lust and love which had clouded her judgement up until now. She saw him as Bella must have seen him. Famous, gorgeous, rich. One of the great playboys who'd had dalliances with some of the most beautiful women in the world. Had she *really* thought she could stand in their shadow for long? Even if he had managed to make her feel better about herself, did she really think she was able to hang onto him? To make him *love* her?

He looked up and met her eyes.

'She's gone,' she said flatly.

'Yes.' There was a pause. 'She's nothing like you, is she?'

'Not really.' Carly forced a smile. 'Were you attracted to her?'

'Was I attracted to her?' he repeated slowly. 'Why do you ask a question like that?'

Carly reminded herself that he had taught her not to have hang-ups about sex, so didn't that mean that she should start thinking about it the way that the rest of the world did? Like some kind of casual exercise to be enjoyed. 'Most men are.'

'Are they?' he said, his tone now ominous. 'What, did you think I wanted to bed your sister, Carly? Or perhaps to live out the fantasy of taking the two of you at the same time?'

Her skin had turned to ice. 'D-did you?'

He gripped his hands into two tight fists, which hung down by the powerful shafts of his thighs, his face darkening like thunder. 'No, I did not,' he gritted out. 'Just what kind of man do you take me for?'

Carly had never seen him so angry. His black eyes were cold and his shadowed jaw looked as hard as granite. 'I know what kind of man you are,' she said. 'Remember?'

'I may have had a chequered past, but I have treated you with nothing but respect since we became lovers,' he ground out. 'I've been up front with you every step of the way and as considerate as I know how. But it seems you couldn't wait to throw it all back in my face by making veiled suggestions that I might enjoy some sordid little tryst with your sister.'

'I didn't—'

'Yes, you damned well did!' Ruthlessly, he cut across her words, advancing towards her as he had done so many times before, only this time his face was not softened by desire. This time it was hard and cold with fury. 'Maybe in the past, my behaviour might have justified you making such a negative judgement because, God knows, I've certainly been no angel. But there are *limits* to what I would consider acceptable behaviour.'

'Luis—'

'Do you really think I would be willing to replicate that kind of massive betrayal, after what I told you about my mother?'

'I'm sorry,' she said woodenly.

'Even if you could think so little of me, do you really think so little of yourself? Haven't you learned anything, Carly? That sex is not wrong and that you can be just as confident and as beautiful as you make up your mind to be.' He shook his head. 'But you're still allowing yourself to be that same scared woman underneath, aren't you? Still so eager to believe the worst about yourself. What's making you do that? Do you miss the cloak of invisibility you wore for so long? Do you find it so terrifying to be out in the real world that you're looking for some excuse to escape from it again?'

She shook her head as his accusations rained down on her like spiky little hailstones. And even though she wanted to blot out what he was saying to her, somehow she was finding it impossible. *Was* she an emotional coward, eager to think the worst about everyone because it was easier that way?

Or was he?

'Maybe you're right,' she said, pushing her hair out of her face. 'But if I'm having difficulty adapting to normality maybe that's because none of this *is* normal. I feel like someone who has jumped into the wrong end of the swimming pool. I'm out of my depth and I don't fit in. Not here. Not anywhere, really.'

'Then *find* your depth,' he said grimly. 'You're an intelligent woman. Don't tell me that you're planning to go to medical school at the age of twenty-three and then start playing the shrinking violet again. You are capable of so much, Carly. Of anything you want, if only you have the courage to reach out and grab it.'

Carly sucked in a deep breath, terrified that tears were going to arrive just when she least needed them. Because although his words were intended as an encouragement—and they were—they were also intended as a farewell. Her lips wobbled for a couple of seconds before she could trust herself to speak. 'You're very good at dishing out advice, aren't you, Luis? But I wonder how good you are at taking it.'

He gave a bitter laugh. 'Why, is this now going to become some kind of tit for tat?'

'It's more about redressing the balance than scoring points,' she said, hating the sarcasm she heard in his drawled response, hating this new distance between them which was growing bigger by the second. 'You wonder why I was so eager to jump to the wrong conclusion about you wanting my sister? Well, why shouldn't I think something like that, when you told me emphatically that you didn't think men were capable of fidelity?'

'Now you're twisting my words.'

'Am I? Or am I just putting my own interpretation on them?' She stared at him. 'Because I don't think that you do believe that, not really. I think that's just your excuse for staying away from commitment.'

'My *excuse*?' he demanded.

'Yes.' Her voice dropped to a whisper. 'I think you were hurt so badly by what happened with your parents. I think you felt completely betrayed by your mother's friend and your father and maybe even by your mother, too, for allowing herself to fade away and leave you. I think the pain was so bad that you vowed never to let anyone get that close to you again. So you didn't. You lived the life you could, the life which was expected of you, the playboy with all the different homes and all the different women. But no matter how many there were it was never enough, was it? They could never fill that hole deep inside you. At the end of the day, you were still all alone. And you always will be if you carry on like this.'

'That's enough!' he bit out and suddenly he wanted to lash out at something. Anything. He wanted to smash his fist into that marble statue on the opposite side of the terrace and see it lie in shattered pieces. He wanted stop the hurt which was enveloping him in something so dark and clammy that suddenly he couldn't breathe properly.

'You may be planning to major in psychology,

but so far you're way off course!' he snapped. 'Is this supposed to make me *want* you, Carly? Am I supposed to be *grateful* for this brutal character assessment of yours? To be so in awe of your unique *insight* that I will somehow see the light? And what do you suppose will happen next, hmm? Play out the scene for me, *querida*, so that I can see it for myself. Do I now drop down onto one knee and ask you to become my wife?'

The breath dying in her throat, Carly stared at him. His caustic words were like having a blade rammed straight into her heart, but she told herself that maybe he'd done her a favour. Because hadn't this liberated her from any dormant hopes she might have nurtured, no matter how much she'd tried to deny them? Wouldn't she now be free of the fantasy that, deep down, Luis might actually *care* about her?

She shook her head. 'I may have been innocent,' she said slowly. 'But I'm not stupid. And if ever I was going to marry anyone it certainly wouldn't be a man who didn't even have the courage to look at himself properly.'

His eyes narrowed. 'You accuse me—*me*— of lacking in courage?'

She shook her head. 'Oh, I'm not talking about the kind of courage which made you put your foot down on the accelerator and take your car through a gap so tiny that most men wouldn't have seen it. I'm talking about the emotional courage to face your demons and put them to rest. Just as I've had to do. I'm sorry I said that about Bella—that was just a lingering hang-up from my own past. I had no right to accuse you of that, and I should have been strong enough to stand up to her.'

But she knew why she hadn't answered Bella's question about her involvement with Luis and why she hadn't dared stand up for herself. Because she didn't believe in the strength of what she and Luis had together. She hadn't wanted to see the pity or the glee in her sister's face when it all ended. And it seemed that her instinct had been right.

'Anyway,' she continued. 'At least this has given us the ending we both knew was inevitable, even if it hasn't been quite as amicable as we might have wanted. We both know that I can't go back to being your housekeeper.'

There was a long pause before he spoke. 'No. I guess you can't.' He flicked her a glance from between narrowed black eyes. 'So what will you do?'

She took a moment to compose herself. To behave as if they'd been talking about nothing more controversial than the weather. And didn't some stupid part of her wish that he'd fought a bit harder to get her to stay? 'I'll find another job until next September. I should have all the funds I need by then to take up my place.'

He frowned. 'But you told me that there was a deferred space available now. So in theory, you could go this September—if you had the funds.'

'Which I don't.'

'You could if I gave them to you. And before you say anything—don't. I can afford it and I want to. Please, Carly. Don't let pride stop you from taking what I am able to give. At least that way, you'll get your happy ending.'

She looked at him and thought that she wasn't the only one who could be naïve. Did he really think that this was her happy ending? She thought about the father who had betrayed him and the mother who had slowly slipped away from the world. She thought about how alone he was, amid all his trophies and homes and enough money in the bank to secure the future of the children he would never have.

And something made her say it. Made her kick her pride into touch and have the courage to declare what she'd known for a long time now. Couldn't she give *him* something, too? Not money, but something much more precious.

Hope.

'Okay, I'll take it. And I want you to know that I am very grateful to you for your…generosity, in all its many forms.' She sucked in a lungful of air but her next words still came out in a breathless rush, full of nerves and apprehension.

'But you should know something else, too, and that is that I've grown to love you, Luis. And I'm sorry about that, because I know it's the last thing you ever wanted. I didn't want to fall in love with you, but, somewhere along the way, I did. And I'm not saying it because I want anything in return, because I don't. I don't expect anything. I'm saying it because, deep down, you *are* loveable. And you need to believe that. It's not because you're sexy, or rich and not because you have a whole room- ful of silver trophies and can fly a plane. You are loveable because you can be a very kind and thoughtful man, when you let yourself be. And maybe one day you might start believ- ing in that enough to open your heart and let someone in.'

Her words died out to the sound of silence. There wasn't a flicker of response from the rigid figure who stood in front of her, though she thought she saw something flare briefly in the depths of those empty black eyes. But then it was gone, and he smiled. That easy, charming smile he could turn on like a tap, a smile which was as cool and as transparent as water itself.

'Interesting hypothesis,' he said, in a voice which sounded faintly bored. 'But you know that I'm not really interested in the emotional stuff you women are so fond of spouting. All I will say, for what it's worth, is that I think you're going to be a brilliant doctor.'

Carly stared at him. *He had completely ignored what she'd just said.* Had treated her words with contempt. Of course he had. Why should she be surprised when he was just being true to himself? He didn't *do* that emotional stuff and he never would. He'd told her that all along.

And it was that which made her quickly turn and walk towards her room, before she added to her humiliation by letting him see her cry.

CHAPTER ELEVEN

LUIS STARED OUT of the window, without really seeing the sombre grey of the November day. Why was he feeling like this? As if there were some heavy weight on his shoulders which was perpetually weighing him down? As if there were something gnawing away inside him, which he couldn't work out how to fix. And that didn't make sense. Especially since he'd kept so busy after putting Carly on a plane back to London and saying goodbye to her.

He had left the Côte d'Azur and travelled to New York, where he'd hired a personal trainer before getting straight back behind the wheel and winning a charity race in Brazil. He remembered staring at the gleaming trophy and thinking it would have been around the same time that Carly was starting at med school in

England. And he couldn't shake off his feeling of disappointment that she hadn't bothered to contact him to say well done.

He knew their relationship was over—he was the one who had ended it, wasn't he?—but the race had been big news internationally, and hadn't he expected some kind of acknowledgement? If not exactly praise, then surely *something*. Perhaps a faintly mocking communication noting that he still seemed hooked on danger, but congratulating him on winning the race, all the same.

But there was nothing.

Not a phone call. Not a postcard.

Nothing.

Never had a silence seemed quite so deafening.

He remembered feeling disbelief, closely followed by a slow and simmering anger. After all he'd done for her she didn't even have the generosity of spirit to say *well done*.

He had buried himself in his work, throwing himself into every new task with the enthusiasm of someone who was just starting out in the cut-throat world of business.

But something inside him had altered. Something he hadn't expected. He found himself looking at things differently. He started making changes he suspected had been a long time coming. He sold two of his houses and a whole heap of office space in Manhattan. He realised that he preferred life without all the hangers-on and so he reduced the size of his entourage, and told Diego so. A Diego who kept looking at him from between narrowed eyes and asking was he *sure* he was okay?

Was he okay? Luis had felt his mouth harden in response to the question. Of course he was. Physically, he'd never felt better. His brush with death had made him look at the world with a sharper focus. His senses felt raw and heightened. In many ways, he had never been so grateful just to be alive.

Yet all he could think about was Carly. Carly lying naked in his arms, with her hair spread over his chest, talking in that soft, sweet way she had. Carly running her finger along his jaw and teasing him. Carly sending him a silent glance, which would make him think about something in a way he hadn't thought about it before.

He tried going to parties to get her out of his head, and there were plenty of parties. Slick, pared-down affairs in minimalist New York loft spaces or wild, pool-side extravaganzas held outside the city.

Trouble was that he couldn't look at a swimming pool without thinking about her.

He couldn't look at a damned bed without thinking about her.

He would find himself standing motionless while some impossibly glamorous woman came onto him in a way which made his stomach crawl. And that was when he started to get worried.

He tried looking at the situation logically. He was only fantasising about her because she'd been like no other lover he'd ever had. Because she had walked away without a backward glance and seemed happy to leave it that way.

Yet she'd been part of his life for a long time, way before they'd become lovers. He told himself he was interested to see how her ambition was playing out—hell, didn't he have some sort of *right* to know?

And now he was back in England on the second round of interviews for a new housekeeper to replace her and it was proving harder than he'd imagined. The first stream of women he'd seen had been hopeless, even though they'd all been eager for the job. But there was something wrong with each and every one of them. Too flirty, or too unimaginative. Several had been no good at cooking and one even had a criminal record she'd tried to conceal. He had rejected them all and demanded that Diego find him someone more suitable.

He looked down at the list of 'more suitable' candidates in front of him. On paper some looked promising, but his heart wasn't in it. He thought how long it had been since he'd eaten a decent *alfajor.* How long since he'd played poker. Or had sex. How long since he'd been made to laugh, or argue or defend himself in the presence of a sharp and amusing mind.

And that was when it hit him, harder than an opponent's wheel flying off during a practice lap.

He didn't want a housekeeper. He didn't want someone to replace Carly, because she was irreplaceable. He wanted... He closed his eyes. He knew what he wanted but it was a big ask. Too big an ask, surely, after what he had done. He flinched as he remembered the way she had looked at him, with that hesitant expression on her face. How she must have met nothing but coldness in his eyes in return. But that hadn't stopped her, had it? She had taken a deep breath and told him she loved him—even though it must have taken an almighty leap of courage and faith to do so. She had hung on in there and said what she needed to say. She had conquered her own insecurity and told him that he was a loveable man. She had done that *because she thought he needed to know.* And how had he reacted? He had treated her declaration with contempt and acted as if she'd said nothing at all.

He shook his head as the door opened and he saw Diego's swarthy features set in a questioning look.

'Shall I show in the first applicant, boss?'

But Luis was already rising to his feet and shaking his head.

'No,' he said fiercely as a powerful sense of resolve washed over him. 'Forget the interviews.'

'But—'

'I said, *forget* them. I have something I need to do.' His heart was pounding as he slid his phone into his pocket and reached for his jacket. 'Somewhere I need to go.'

He drove down to Southampton in his bright red car, only just staying inside the speed limit. The sky was low and the air filled with drizzle and, even though it was only late morning, all the cars on the motorway had their headlights turned on so that shafts of golden light cut through the sombre greyness.

The medical school was situated in a green swathe of land on the edge of the city and it was nearly lunchtime by the time Luis finally parked up. He turned up the collar of his leather coat as hordes of students streamed past him and as he looked into all the unknown faces he wondered why the hell he hadn't bothered to call her first.

You know why you haven't called her.

Because she might just have told you to go to hell, and you just might have deserved it.

He made his way to some reception office and saw the girl behind the desk turn very pink when he asked where he might find a first-year student called Carly Conner.

'We're…we're not really allowed to give out that sort of information,' she stumbled.

He leaned over the desk and used a smile which had never failed him. 'Do you think your medical school would like a substantial donation?'

She nodded.

'Then why don't you tell me where I might find Carly Conner?'

He was informed that the first-year medical students were on their way to lunch and the girl hadn't finished giving him directions before he was weaving across some courtyard towards a cafeteria, which was packed with crowds of students.

And that was when he saw her.

At first he almost didn't recognise her, because she looked *different*. As if she belonged. She was laughing and talking to a small nucleus of people, a bag loaded with books slung over her shoulder.

He felt the clench of his heart as he stood stock-still and watched her and maybe somebody noticed him because suddenly heads were turning in his direction. Across the crowded courtyard he saw the colour drain from Carly's face as she looked up and met his gaze.

She didn't move and, at first, neither did he. He felt as if the blood had frozen in his veins and he would be stuck to that spot for ever. And then he began walking towards her, his legs feeling heavy and wooden and somehow disassociated from him.

The students with her had formed themselves into a protective semicircle and Luis automatically picked out some young Adonis with hair like buttered corn and eyes of startling blue, who seemed to be unconsciously squaring up his shoulders as Luis approached.

She tilted her chin as he got closer and now he could see why she looked so different. She had changed in ways which were both subtle yet startling. Her hair was still long, but now it was weaved into a complex plait which hung down over one shoulder. And she was wearing *make-up.* Luis swallowed. Not much, just a lick of mascara and a slick of something which was making her lips gleam. She looked…amazing.

In her jeans and short jacket she somehow managed to fade into the crowd and yet to stand out from it. And instantly, he understood why she had refused to take the expensive clothes he'd bought her, for she would have no use for them here, in her new life. His heart clenched as he thought of the yellow and white spotted dress still hanging in the wardrobe of his French home. Of the space beside him in a bed which had never seemed empty before she had gone and left it.

'Hello, Carly,' he said.

Her expression was wary as she looked at him. She didn't look exactly overjoyed. In fact, that was an understatement. Her face had grown pale and tight and her eyes were cool.

'I'm not going to ask why you're here,' she said in a low voice. 'Because obviously you've decided you wanted to see me, but you really might have given me some warning, Luis.'

He was not expecting a reprimand and for a moment he was...*shocked*. He thought how any other woman would have hurled herself into his arms and the slight deflation he felt was almost certainly something to do with his ego. *And mightn't that be a good thing?* he questioned with a self-awareness which suddenly made him feel uncomfortable.

'I thought that if I'd warned you, you might have refused to see me,' he said, his gaze training hard on her face. 'Would you?'

She shrugged as if she didn't really care. 'I don't know.'

'You need any help, Carl?'

The Adonis had stepped forward and Luis held onto his temper with difficulty as Carly shook her head again.

'No, I'm fine,' she said.

'I need to speak to you, Carly,' said Luis softly, flicking a dismissive glance towards the youth. 'In private.'

For a moment she hesitated. He saw emotions he didn't recognise, and some he did, crossing those iced-tea eyes, before she looked down at her watch.

'I've got half an hour before my next lecture, so you'll have to be quick.'

'I thought you were never on time.'

'That was in the old days. I've changed.' Defiantly, she met his eyes. 'We can walk in the grounds. Come with me.'

He was barely aware of the total silence which suddenly descended on the courtyard, or the excited chatter which rose up before they were barely out of earshot. The grass was sodden beneath their feet as they left the courtyard and the bare branches of the trees were etched in forbidding lines against the low sky.

'What are you doing here, Luis?' Her breath was like a cloud of smoke as it billowed out into the cold air.

He swallowed. He hadn't really planned what he was going to say because hadn't some cynical side of his nature wondered whether this might just turn out to be a form of catharsis. That he would take one look at her and wonder what all the fuss had been about. Why he'd been unable to sleep or to think of anything much which didn't involve Carly Conner with her clever mind and soft body and that way of prising out secrets he'd locked away from everyone else.

But it wasn't turning out that way. It was as he had suspected all along. His heart was tight in his chest, as if an iron band were squeezing all the blood out of it, and his pulse was racing with a feeling which felt like excitement and exultation and apprehension all rolled into one. He'd experienced something like it when he'd been waiting on the starting line at the notoriously tough twenty-four-hour race at Le Mans, or any of the other myriad dangerous racetracks he'd tackled during his race career, but nothing like this. *Nothing like this.*

He stared into eyes as cold as chips of ice and suddenly it all came spilling out from a place deep inside him. 'I love you,' he said simply and waited for her reaction as he repeated the words in a voice he'd never heard himself use before. 'I love you, Carly Conner.'

Carly shook her head and her hands clenched into tight fists. She wished she hadn't forgotten her gloves because then she could have avoided her fingernails digging into her flesh like this. But the sharp pain helped her focus on her anger, and anger was the safest thing she had to hang onto right then. She glared at him. How dared he do this? How dared he come here and disrupt the life which she was building for herself—day by day? How dared he, by coming out with something he probably didn't mean, undo all her good work of trying to forget him? How dared he come here and try to *break her heart* all over again?

'You don't "do" love,' she snapped. 'Remember? It's top of your list of requirements for lovers—that they won't dare to expect anything like that from you. No wedding bells or clouds of confetti for you. *Your words,* Luis. And I don't have time for meaningless declarations. If you're missing sex then f-find someone else. That shouldn't be a problem for someone like you.'

She made to walk away but his hand reached out and caught her arm and she wanted to shake him off, but she couldn't. *How could he do that?* she wondered desperately. How would her physiology lecturer explain it? How could just one touch from a man make you defy all your instincts? Send your pulse rocketing and fill your mind with thoughts you were intent on not having...

'You're right. I didn't *do* love,' he agreed, still holding onto her arm. 'Because it has never happened to me before. I never thought it could. I'd only ever seen love as a negative. As dark and destructive. As full of pain and lies and betrayal. I didn't realise that it could make you feel a part of something bigger than yourself. Could make you feel as if you were really alive. And you showed me that, Carly. You showed me that like nobody else ever could.'

'Stop it,' she whispered. 'Please, Luis. Just go away.'

He shook his head. 'I'm not going anywhere until you've heard what I've got to say. I miss you more than any words can say. Nothing seems to make sense without you there, and I was a fool to let you go.'

'You didn't *let me go*,' she said. 'You pushed me away. You know you did.'

'Yes, I did,' he said heavily. 'I hold my hands up to that. So maybe it follows that I don't deserve your love, Carly. That I shouldn't be given a second chance, because I threw it all back in your face.' He swallowed. 'So if you tell me that you no longer love me and that you don't want me in your life, then I'll turn around and walk away from here and I will never bother you again. I give you my word on that.'

She stared at him and sucked in a deep breath. 'I don't love you.'

His eyes narrowed. 'I don't believe you.'

'You arrogant bastard.'

'If you didn't love me, then you wouldn't be looking at me like that. Your eyes wouldn't be asking me to hold you properly, nor your lips parting because you want me to kiss them.'

'Luis—'

'And I want that too, *querida*. So much. I want to kiss you and never stop.'

She stared at him and her mouth was trembling but not nearly as much as his hands as he reached out to pull her into his arms. 'Answer me honestly, that's all I ask. Do you still love me, Carly Conner?' he growled. 'Will you marry me and have my babies?'

'Babies?'

She pulled away from him and he saw her frown, like someone who was preparing for a cloud to burst on top of their head. 'But I'm going to be a doctor, Luis. I've worked hard to get here and I'm not going to give it up. I've got six long years of training ahead of me. Six years of me being based in the south of England, while you continue with your jet-setting life elsewhere? Is that going to work out? I don't think so.'

'You don't think it's possible?' He gave a low laugh. 'Believe me, anything is possible if you want it enough. And I want you more than I have ever wanted anything. I respect your ambition and I am prepared to work around it, to support you in whatever you want to do. Because while I can see that there are practical difficulties to be overcome, they are completely irrelevant. There is only one thing which is important and that is my next question and I think you owe it to me to answer it truthfully.' His voice quietened. 'Do you still love me, Carly?'

Carly didn't speak, at least not straight away. It was as if she recognised that her world was going to change irrevocably, no matter what she answered. She became aware of the loudness of her heartbeat and, incongruously, the fact that her leather boots were sinking into the muddy grass. She could see the bare trees which surrounded them and in the sky a dark flock of birds who were heading somewhere. She wondered where. To their own warmer future? She saw Luis's expression: his eyes were narrowed and the lines etched along the sides of his unsmiling mouth were deeper than she remembered. The faint drizzle had settled on his black hair—so that it seemed to have covered the tangled tendrils like a fine mist of diamonds.

She thought about the tears she had shed since

she'd left France. About the great, gaping hole where her heart used to be. She thought about how much she'd missed their sparring. His teasing. And a million things in between.

She thought about the practical difficulties which lay ahead if she told him what he really seemed to want to hear. Of how on earth they might be able to align two obviously incompatible lifestyles to any degree of satisfaction.

And then she remembered what he had just said.

Anything is possible. And with Luis, she honestly believed it was.

She nodded, her mouth working furiously as she tried to control the emotions which were building up inside her and threatening to spill out. *I am not going to cry,* she told herself fiercely. *Because I have an anatomy lecture to get to.*

'Yes, I love you, Luis Martinez,' she blurted out. 'I tried very hard not to, but in the end I couldn't help myself.'

'Couldn't you?' he questioned softly.

'No. You were like a fever to which there was no known antidote and once you'd got into my blood, I couldn't seem to get rid of you. I still can't.'

'That bad, huh?' Tenderly, he smiled. 'That's not the most romantic declaration I've ever heard, but it's certainly the most original. Just like you, my clever, sweet Carly.'

And that was when the tears came and there was nothing she could do to stop them. They spilled down her cheeks and dripped onto the collar of her jacket, like giant drops of rain.

But Luis was there to dry them and Luis was there to kiss her and once they started kissing, they couldn't seem to stop, and Carly's heart seemed to burst out of her chest as he gathered her in his arms and held her.

She touched his shoulders, his hair and his face, as if she couldn't quite believe he was there. But he was. Every vital, warm, living and breathing atom of him. *He was there. With her.* And if she was to believe what he was telling her, which against all the odds she did, he wasn't ever going to leave her again.

She made it to her anatomy class, with seconds to spare.

EPILOGUE

'ARE YOU AWAKE?'

Carly gave a slow and luxurious wriggle as her eyelashes fluttered open to meet the soft question in Luis's black gaze. 'I am now.'

Dark brows arched upwards. 'Did I wake you?'

'Wasn't that your intention when you started playing with my breasts like that?'

He smiled. 'Do you want me to stop?'

She sighed and closed her eyes. 'What do you think?'

'I think you're endlessly fascinating, Dr Martinez, and I love you very much. And I want you to know that these last six years have been the best of my life.'

Her eyes fluttered open and she bit her lip with expectation, never tiring of hearing him say these words. 'Really?'

'You know they have, *querida.*'

Yes, she knew. Just as they had been for her.

It hadn't been easy to rearrange Luis's life to accommodate her demanding role as a medical student, but then she'd discovered that the best things in life always had to be fought for. And Luis wanted her to achieve her dream as much as she did. He told her how proud he was of what she'd done and what she'd achieved, in spite of all the odds being stacked against her.

These days, he travelled as little as possible and had made his main base in England. From their sprawling Hampshire estate with its easy proximity to the sea, he now masterminded his latest business success—three ocean-going cruise ships as well as a flourishing yacht business. As for the rest of his global concerns, somewhere along the way he had become—as Carly told him with some pride—a consummate delegator. He employed the best people who gave of their best—and consequently the Martinez foundation had evolved, and was flourishing.

And even though he never really grew to *love* the English climate, he made sure he took them on plenty of sunny and luxurious vacations to compensate. Which was why Carly could often be found reading a haematology textbook on the beach, beside the clear aqua waters of the Caribbean.

She sighed, feeling Luis's thumb tracing enticing little circles over her nipple. From the window a clear river of light flooded in, illuminating the large bed in which they lay. She loved their home. They had bought a house overlooking the water not far from the medical school, from where she had graduated last week with honours.

But before the graduation ceremony had come their wedding, a wedding which Carly had resolutely refused to consider while she'd been in the middle of her studies. It had driven Luis crazy. For someone who had shied away from matrimony all his adult life, it had become one of his fiercest ambitions to wed her. The trouble was that he'd fallen in love with a woman who seemed resistant to wearing his ring.

'But you don't believe that men can do fidelity, remember?' she had flung at him, only half teasingly.

'Wrong tense,' he had growled back. 'I didn't—until I met you!'

The more he tried to persuade her to change her mind, the firmer she stood, but in a funny kind of way that had only made him love her more.

She had finally agreed to become his wife just before she graduated, telling him that she wanted to bear his name and to be Dr Martinez. And that simple declaration had thrilled him in a way which had left him shaken.

They had married in a small grey chapel overlooking one of Hampshire's green valleys and Carly had worn white roses in her hair and a simple dress, which had whispered over the flaggedstoned floor as she had walked to the altar to greet him.

Bella had been there, her initial poorly disguised jealousy at Carly's fate suddenly eclipsed by the presence of Luis's jet-setting friends at the ceremony. The Sultan of Qurhah was in attendance, with his beautiful wife and their gorgeous new baby. Niccolo Da Conti and Alekto Sarantos were easily considered to be the best-looking men there and the fact that they both happened to be billionaires only added to their appeal as far as Bella was concerned.

'Good luck with that,' Luis commented drily to his bride as he watched her sister slink across the room towards Niccolo, in a dress so tight that he privately wondered how she was managing to walk.

Carly turned in the direction of his gaze. 'But he's single, isn't he?'

'Yes, he's single.' Luis laughed. 'But if you think *I* was a commitment-phobe, let me tell you that Niccolo Da Conti takes the concept into a whole new stratosphere!'

'And you turned out to be the least commitment-phobic man on the planet!'

'Only because I met the only woman who could change my mind.'

'Oh, Luis.'

'Oh, Carly,' he murmured indulgently.

Her mother had been there, too; a mother amazed by Carly's 'luck' in finding herself such a rich husband. And if Carly was disappointed not to have been commended for working her way through med school—she kept it to herself. She'd learnt that there were some things you could never change and therefore it was a waste of time even trying.

She'd learnt so much, along with the demands of medical science.

That her love for Luis grew stronger with every day that passed and that she wanted to have his baby before too long.

That a man whose heart had been wounded only needed the constant love of a woman to repair it. And that love was boundless and limitless.

She'd learnt that sometimes things happened which you wouldn't have even dared to dream about. She was living that dream and so was Luis. He didn't want a life in the fast lane any more. His days as 'The Love Machine' were over. He told her that he'd never really believed that one woman could be everything for one man.

But now he did.

'Come here,' he growled softly. 'I have something I need you to hear.'

Carly smiled as she turned her face to his. 'What is it?'

'I love you,' he said, his arms tightening around her waist. And then he said it again in Spanish just before he kissed her.

* * * * *

Mills & Boon® Large Print

January 2015

THE HOUSEKEEPER'S AWAKENING
Sharon Kendrick

MORE PRECIOUS THAN A CROWN
Carol Marinelli

CAPTURED BY THE SHEIKH
Kate Hewitt

A NIGHT IN THE PRINCE'S BED
Chantelle Shaw

DAMASO CLAIMS HIS HEIR
Annie West

CHANGING CONSTANTINOU'S GAME
Jennifer Hayward

THE ULTIMATE REVENGE
Victoria Parker

INTERVIEW WITH A TYCOON
Cara Colter

HER BOSS BY ARRANGEMENT
Teresa Carpenter

IN HER RIVAL'S ARMS
Alison Roberts

FROZEN HEART, MELTING KISS
Ellie Darkins

1214 Rom LP

MILLS & BOON®
Large Print – February 2015

AN HEIRESS FOR HIS EMPIRE
Lucy Monroe

HIS FOR A PRICE
Caitlin Crews

COMMANDED BY THE SHEIKH
Kate Hewitt

THE VALQUEZ BRIDE
Melanie Milburne

THE UNCOMPROMISING ITALIAN
Cathy Williams

PRINCE HAFIZ'S ONLY VICE
Susanna Carr

A DEAL BEFORE THE ALTAR
Rachael Thomas

THE BILLIONAIRE IN DISGUISE
Soraya Lane

THE UNEXPECTED HONEYMOON
Barbara Wallace

A PRINCESS BY CHRISTMAS
Jennifer Faye

HIS RELUCTANT CINDERELLA
Jessica Gilmore